After leaving the res [...]
and slipped into his [...]
the clip and shucked [...]
remove any excess [...]
and he didn't like th [...]
hadn't liked the feel of the one that [...]
back, either.

He stayed in his room with the light off. Sunset flared in the west like the fires of an Indian massacre. He waited until the light faded, then put on a sports jacket, buttoned it, and went out trying to look like a man with a heavy dinner rather than a .45 automatic under his belt.

As he walked, his imagination started to give him a bad time. The window curtains of houses seemed to quiver as if people were spying on him. Odd rustlings trailed him down the street and halted abruptly when he jerked his head around to see what was causing them. When he reached the garage, lights were on in the repair shop and the overhead doors were up. Off in one corner a big guy in coveralls was working at a bench.

The guy's back looked like a wonderful target. His own back must have looked that way just before the slug tore into it. Maybe he ought to think about drilling Russ right now, while his back was turned. Why was it worse to shoot a man in the back than in the front? The result was the same. In fact it was probably the humane thing to do because it was all over before the guy knew what hit him. Lots of guys had been shot in the back and hadn't objected to it.

Nobody else was in sight, and the nearest house was a block away. He got out the automatic and jacked a cartridge into the chamber...

Say It With
BULLETS

by **Richard Powell**

A HARD CASE CRIME NOVEL

A HARD CASE CRIME BOOK
(HCC-018)
March 2006

Published by

Dorchester Publishing Co., Inc.
200 Madison Avenue
New York, NY 10016

in collaboration with Winterfall LLC

ISBN 0-8439-5589-9

The name "Hard Case Crime" and the Hard Case Crime logo
are trademarks of Winterfall LLC. Hard Case Crime books are
selected and edited by Charles Ardai.

Printed in the United States of America

Visit us on the web at www.HardCaseCrime.com

SAY IT WITH BULLETS

One

At the overnight stop in North Platte, Nebraska, Bill Wayne didn't copy the other tourists in the party when they bought postcards to mail to friends. He was running a little low on friends these days. Once he had classed five guys as friends but they had picked up a habit of doing things behind his back, like shooting at it. The only wish-you-were-here postcard he wanted to send them was a picture of a cemetery.

Among the queer angles of the case was the fact that he didn't know exactly why the shooting had started. He was on his way now to visit his former pals and ask how come. In case they didn't feel like answering he had brought a .45 automatic to talk for him.

In his hotel room that night he unpacked the automatic so he could practice drawing it fast. He stuck the gun under his belt and walked over to the full-length door mirror. Once upon a time mirrors had shown him a happy-go-lucky face that grinned easily and foolishly at people. This was a very different face. Under rumpled black hair were eyebrows linked in a frown, eyes that looked around restlessly for trouble, a thin tight mouth, chin set in hard lines. Not a pretty face. It would only look good on a police WANTED poster, and that was where it would end up if he wasn't careful.

He stood there and practiced drawing the automatic. The results were disgusting. You might think he was trying to outfumble somebody in reaching for a nightclub check. He would have to do better than that. He practiced for several hours and then went to bed and had one of those dreams in which you shoot and shoot at a guy but the bullets have no effect.

In the morning he climbed wearily into the bus and took his usual seat alone in the rear and tried to catch a nap. It didn't work. As the bus skimmed westward, little jolts flipped up from the rear wheels and jarred his body. Now and then one of the jolts plucked an echo from his rib cage as if a bass viol string had been strummed. That would be where the slug had ripped through him a few years ago in China. Now and then he got another twinge on his left side, where a bullet had nicked him last month in Philadelphia. You could call it a homecoming present. Quite probably the same guy had shot him both times. They might all be in on it, though. There was Russ who now lived in Cheyenne, and Ken in Salt Lake City and Frankie in Reno and Cappy in San Francisco and Domenic in Los Angeles.

It was convenient that they had settled down in those places after returning from China. It meant he could cover up his trail perfectly, in going to visit them, by hanging a camera around his neck and an open-mouthed expression on his face and playing tourist. He could ask all kinds of questions without raising suspicions. He had even been able to shop around for a packaged vacation tour that hit all those spots, and to let a travel agency make all the reservations and supply him with a crowd to hide in. The agency that was carting him and his .45 tenderly across the country was called Treasure Trips, Inc., and he was on a tour called Treasure Trip of the Old West, $750 plus tax. Not counting the tax, that worked out to $150 per friend.

The bus whipped past a highway sign that said: Cheyenne 207 miles.

Hello, Russ, he thought. Here I come ready or not. Here—

He glanced up and saw that, ready or not, he was going to have a visitor. A girl was coming down the aisle with an easy flowing walk that made you think of a flag in a breeze. Treasure Trips, Inc., tried to keep its patrons happy. If you tired of looking at scenery outside the bus you could look at Holly Clark inside it. She was the hostess-courier. Unfortunately no provision was made for a guy who had no interest either in scenery or in Miss Clark. She would come back and probably ask if he was comfortable and was he enjoying the trip and would he like a pillow for the back of his head.

He wished people would let him alone. It used to be that he liked people. Not any more, though. It did something to you when you went through a war with five guys you trusted and afterward teamed up with them in starting a business and then suddenly collected a shot in the back. It made you look at everybody suspiciously. Of course there were plenty of people in the world who were okay, but he no longer had any confidence in his ability to pick them out. When anybody tried to get friendly with him now he kept trying to figure out their angle. Like this girl, for instance. Why did she try to give him so much attention when he had shown clearly that he didn't want any? What was her angle?

She came back to him and instead of the usual smile gave him a frown. "You sit back here with the angriest look on your face," she said. "Do you know what you remind me of? Of a tornado getting ready to wreck something. Is something the matter?"

"Everything's fine. You don't have to worry about me."

"But it's part of my job to worry, if somebody doesn't seem to be enjoying the trip. Aren't we taking good care of you? Don't you like the other people in our party or the scenery or anything?"

Maybe if he was rude she would go away. "The trouble with the scenery in Nebraska," he said, "is that it doesn't hide the landscape."

She said earnestly, "It may be a little flat, but you ought to think how historic it is. Why, right along here was the Mormon Trail. And the Oregon Trail. And the route of the Pony Express. You're riding through history!"

"I'll try to get in the spirit of things. Don't be surprised if I start picking off redskins and yelling Californy er bust."

"Frankly," she said, "I think you're more the type who would have picked on settlers. A few minutes ago I was watching you stare at the scenery and honestly, you looked as if you were choosing a spot to ambush the next stagecoach."

That knocked him off balance. He hadn't broken so much as a traffic law but already this girl was tagging him as one of the James boys. In view of his future plans, he'd better do something about that. Perhaps if he made a quiet, gentlemanly pass at her, she would forget that ambush business. Or anyway translate it into more ordinary terms. He tried to remember how you made a pass at a girl like Holly Clark. He had been out of the country for a good many years and his technique was rusty.

He forced his face into a grin, and said, "You've got me wrong. I was probably choosing a spot to ambush the next blonde. By the way, you're one, aren't you? Quite a coincidence."

"This is the third day we've been on this bus. You've just discovered I'm a blonde. If it takes you that long merely to spot a blonde I don't think you'll ambush many."

"The way you do your hair fooled me. I mean, pulling it straight back and tying it in that horsetail effect. Makes you look more prim than I expect a blonde to be. Sort of like a schoolmarm."

"This is a very popular type of hairdo nowadays," she said indignantly. "And just by the way, I don't like that word—schoolmarm. Because I happen to be a school teacher."

"I will be right over to take a course."

"You'll fit in nicely. I teach first grade."

"Since there are only two people in this conversation," he said, "I think I am coming off no worse than second best. So you bully little children nine months of the year and push tourists like me around the rest of the time, do you?"

"Any time I can borrow a bulldozer, Mr. Wayne, I'll try to push you around. May I sit down? I'd like to ask a couple of questions."

He shoved over against the window, and grumbled, "You've already asked a couple of questions and I seem to get zeros on the answers. However…"

She sat beside him and tilted her head to one side and studied him as if he were something small and wiggly on a slide under a microscope. She had wide gray eyes and a nice mouth and firm chin and a nose that was in remarkably good shape, considering the way it kept poking into other people's business. She wasn't very old and probably she ought to be attending classes instead of holding them. He reminded himself not to scowl at her; he was supposed to be making a pass at the girl.

"Exactly why," she said, "did you come on this trip?"

"I had seven hundred and fifty bucks, plus tax, and some time to waste. Why does anybody come on it?"

"Most people want to see the country. Do you?"

"Well, not right here, maybe. But I'm looking forward to some of the sights later on."

"What sights, Mr. Wayne?"

He wasn't prepared for a cross-examination like this. He had assumed that people would let him alone and not ask pointed questions. He had maps and a lot of information about Cheyenne and Salt Lake City and Reno and San Francisco and L.A., but he didn't want to show any special interest in those places. "I'm looking forward," he said, "to seeing Yosemite National Park."

"Wonderful! And what especially are you looking forward to seeing in Yosemite?"

Yosemite...Yosemite...what the devil was at Yosemite? He took a stab at it, and said, "I expect Old Faithful will be interesting."

She smiled sweetly at him, "It certainly will be, if it has managed to move there from Yellowstone National Park."

Nice work, Wayne. You just flunked first-year geography. "This is bad," he said. "You'd better keep me after school."

"I don't want you to think I'm rude, asking all those questions," she said earnestly, "but I have a job to do. My job is to run the trip smoothly and make sure everybody enjoys it. One person who doesn't like the trip can throw everything out of gear. So I worry when you sit alone with that grim look on your face. And you're so different from everybody else in the party that I don't quite know how to handle the problem."

"What makes me so different?"

"For one thing, you don't happen to be middle-aged."

He looked around the bus. He had never realized before that it was a middle-aged crowd. There was just one young person in the bunch: a thin-faced girl of about twenty who wore glasses and a resigned look and was traveling with her mother. "Don't let appearances fool you," he said. "Some days I feel eighty."

"What a ridiculous statement!" she cried. "You were just thirty years old last November and—"

His right hand moved before he could think. It grabbed her wrist, fingers biting into her flesh. He glared into her shocked eyes and said, "How did you find that out? What's your angle?"

"Let my wrist go, please."

His fingers unclenched slowly. He had been out of the country for almost ten years. He had come back to a land where nearly everybody was a stranger except five guys who wanted to kill him. So it was quite a jolt to find somebody had collected a fact or two about his background. "Sorry," he muttered. "I'd still like to know what your game is."

"All right," she said. "My game is football. It used to be yours, too. And your coach was Rocky Clark."

"Clark...that's your name, isn't it? Where do you fit in?"

"Don't you remember?"

He tried to look back into his memory. There were a few old snapshots tucked away in it. Gothic spires in the haze of Indian summer...the River Field on weekdays with footballs tumbling in the sky...the roaring stands on Saturdays...Rocky Clark's red face in the locker room at the half, when they had been taking a pounding. No snapshot of Holly Clark, though. "I can't get it," he said.

She sighed. "I shouldn't have made that slip about your birthday. I was hoping you'd remember me all by yourself. I had it planned. You were going to look at me and say in the most delighted tone, 'Why, you were that pretty little kid of Rocky Clark's who used to tag around after me all the time.' "

He studied her face. If you gave her bangs and a Dutch bob, and plumped out her face and body, and put bands on her teeth and—"Oh, sure," he said. "You were only what, twelve or thirteen? And what do you mean, pretty little kid? You were a fat lump."

"That's a fine reward. You were my hero and I was just a fat lump to you. I used to cheer everything you did on the field."

"Your father didn't teach you much football, then. You should have booed."

"You were very good," she said indignantly. "After all, you were only a sophomore that last fall. You enlisted right after Pearl Harbor, didn't you? I don't suppose you ever knew that I put up a service flag in your honor in my room. You were going to come back covered with medals and I was going to marry you."

He wished he knew how to turn this off. He didn't want to play Old Home Week with her or anyone. The less people knew about him, the better. "Kids get funny ideas," he said.

"Well, anyway, you see why I've been acting so interested in you. Bill, why did it upset you so much when I mentioned your birthday?"

When he was packing for the trip he should have included a spare head; the one he was using now didn't seem to be much good. Quick, Wayne, what's a good reason to explain why you're acting like a hunted man? Ah! Nervous breakdown. That would explain why he was taking this trip, too.

He said, "I had sort of a nervous breakdown. That's why I'm jumpy. The doctor told me to take a quiet trip somewhere. I don't like boats so I picked a bus trip."

"Oh, I'm sorry! I suppose you'd been working too hard."

"Yeah, maybe."

"You're not married, of course, or you wouldn't be taking a trip like this alone. Where do you live now, Bill? And what do you do?"

He had to cut this off, but fast. He wasn't ready with the answers to her quiz program. "What I mainly do," he said, "is mind my own business. It's a nice field to be in. Not many people know how to do it."

It was like kicking her in the teeth. She swallowed a couple of times, and then said brightly, "I asked for that, didn't I? I'm a big girl now and ought to stop tagging around after you." She got up and left.

Two

A highway sign flicked some words at him: Cheyenne
176 miles. The miles were peeling off the signs fast. It
gave him the same tight hot feeling in his stomach that
you got trying to keep a crippled plane in the air and
watching your last thousand feet melt off the altimeter.
Except that in this case he wasn't coming closer and
closer to a crash. He was coming closer and closer to
Russ Nordhoff in Cheyenne.

He hoped Russ would talk. He hoped the guy would
open up and give him the whole story and be able to
prove that somebody else had done the shooting.
Otherwise he had better put a slug in Russ. He
thought about that and felt sweat begin crawling over
his body. He had never killed anyone. It was one thing
to practice quick draws in front of a mirror but it
might be very different to look at big dumb Russ along
the barrel of a loaded .45 and squeeze the trigger. He
wished he knew whether he could do it.

Thinking about Russ was getting him wound up too
tight and he stared out of the bus window and tried to
make his mind go blank. The flat Nebraska land was
shimmering in the heat. Houses and barns lost their
outlines and changed shape. The blades of a gaunt

windmill blurred and began looking like the prop of an airplane. Of an old beat-up C-47 that he had flown in China before the Reds came. It was a good plane, though. He had flown it a lot of missions over the Himalayas—the Hump—during the war. Then after the war he and five other guys from his outfit bought it as surplus and had started a little airline in China. They were going to make a million bucks...

This was certainly a swell way to blank out his mind.

He squeezed his eyes shut to see if that would work. A lot of bright dots whirled in his head and then slowed and began painting a picture for him, like dots on a radarscope.

No, that wouldn't work either. His memory was once more digging up that business at Nanking Airfield in 1949. For a moment he almost decided to open his eyes and get rid of the picture, but then he figured he would take another look at it. There was quite a fascination about seeing it each time because it was like a movie, and he kept hoping that some day the camera would make a mistake and show him what had happened behind his back.

He kept his eyes shut and let the picture sharpen. There they were, all five of them: Frankie and Domenic and Russ and Cappy and Ken. His five partners. They had just crossed him up, but good. It was late April of 1949; the Red armies were closing in on Nanking and the Nationalists were clearing out. He and his five pals were clearing out, too. He had told the others to round up a bunch of refugees to take along. Then he had gone into the city to finish some business and when he got back he found his partners had rounded up one refugee. Quite a refugee, too. Nanking's top black market operator. The plane was also loaded with a lot of boxes marked with Chinese characters saying they were medical supplies, and the Chinese black market guy was hovering over them as if he expected an epidemic.

He had kicked the guy off the plane and gone into their operations shack to have it out with his partners. He hadn't gotten to first base.

Ken had said, "So what if this Chink is in the black market? He'll pay ten times what a whole load of refugees will pay, if we fly him to Hong Kong."

"The way I figured," Russ said, "we got to look after ourselves."

"We were gonna make a million, remember?" Domenic said. "We were gonna do it on the level. But every time we made some real dough, this lousy Chinese money dropped in value and we ended with nickels. This is our last chance to cash in."

"We been out here almost four years since the war," Frankie said. "I don't want to go home broke."

"This junk you give us about saving lives," Cappy said. "What if we do leave a lot of refugees? We're flying out all them boxes of medical supplies, ain't we? Ain't that gonna save lives?"

He could have taken everything except that stuff

about medical supplies. He said angrily, "I'm going out and break open those boxes. And you know what? If they're medical supplies, you can kick my teeth in and use some on me."

His memory showed him the way they had stared back at him. Frankie leaned against the wall, watching him sideways out of faded blue eyes. Domenic sat on the edge of a desk, swinging one leg. His heavy-lidded black eyes seemed faintly amused. Big dumb Russ was frowning. Russ had gray eyes that blinked as if they found it hard to understand some of the things they saw. Cappy was mad. His brown eyes had the look of a guy picking a target for a right-hand swing. Ken's eyes were hot, black, excited.

Right after his memory took that picture, he turned and marched out of the operations shack heading for the C-47. He had marched five steps when a slug from a .45 caught up with him and slammed him face down in the dust.

He studied the five pairs of eyes, trying for the hundredth time to figure which pair had looked down the barrel of the .45 at his retreating back. He couldn't get the answer. The picture never gave him a hint of what had happened behind his back. As he studied it the picture faded until there was nothing but five pairs of eyes, watching him, watching...

He opened his eyes and yanked his thoughts back to the present. He had brought something with him out of the past, though. He brought a feeling that somebody was watching him now, years later, on the bus zooming across Nebraska.

He sat very quietly without turning his head or moving his eyes and tried to figure out who it was. Nobody in the front part of the bus was watching him. The seat across from him was empty, and that left only the seat back of him across the rear of the bus. Usually no one sat there. He counted the people he could see: the driver, Holly Clark, thirty passengers. There ought to be thirty-one passengers in sight. One of them was behind him, watching. It made the back of his neck twitch.

He jerked his head around suddenly and caught the guy at it. The watcher was sitting a little off to one side. He was a man in his fifties, with a round face and pink bald head and eyes that you might describe as kindly if you hadn't caught them spying.

"Hello there," the man said. "Finished your nap?"

"Yeah," Bill said.

"I moved back here to get away from all the chatter up front. My wife and two other women are busy trying to dig up mutual acquaintances. They couldn't track them down more grimly if they were detectives hunting a murderer. By the way, I've never met you properly. I'm Brown. Dr. Brown. General practice, in Columbus, Ohio. You're Wayne, I think."

"Yeah."

"Mind if I move up beside you and chat awhile?"

"Yeah," Bill said.

"You mean you do mind?"

"That's right."

The doctor gave an embarrassed laugh. "I'd better make a confession," he said. "I didn't come back here to get away from the chatter. I came back to take a look at you."

"I could feel you watching me."

"A lot of people claim they can feel people watching them, but I don't really think it's true. Your subconscious mind probably took in the fact that somebody walked past you and sat down here. When you awoke, that fact moved into your conscious mind and was translated into a feeling that you were being watched."

"Very interesting. Where does that leave us, Doc?"

"Well. I ought to explain. That nice girl, Miss Clark, was talking to me a short time ago. It seems she used to know you way back when. She said you'd come on this trip to get over a nervous breakdown, and she was worried about you and didn't think you were getting over it and wondered if I could help."

Bill said disgustedly, "You know how you can help? You can go to work on her. She's got a bad case of minding other people's business. I don't know if it's curable."

Brown chuckled and said, "You may be right. Nice girl, though. Matter of fact I wouldn't have taken any action on what she told me except that my wife and I had the room next to yours last night. You may remember the walls in that hotel were thin, and I woke up a few times and heard you pacing around. And this morning I could see you hadn't slept much."

"Lots of people don't sleep well sometimes."

"This is very unprofessional of me, Wayne. But if there's anything I can do, just on a friendly basis—"

"You want my case history, Doc?"

"If you'd like to tell me."

Bill smiled. He wondered what the guy would say if he gave him the straight dope. It might go like this:

I don't sleep well at night, Doc, because I just got back from hiding out in Red China for four years. Back in '49 some pals of mine pumped a slug into my back and left me for dead. Some Chinese nursed me back to what we will laughingly call health, and then I started keeping one jump ahead of the Reds.

I got home to Philly a couple months ago and began sleeping better. But by lousy luck one of the newspapers printed a story about me escaping from Red China and I guess those pals of mine got to read it somehow and found I wasn't dead. A week after the story ran, somebody took another shot at me at night in front of my family's house. So now I don't sleep well anymore.

But I have a cure all worked out, Doc. I'm on my way to visit my old pals. I hadn't figured on bothering them but if they won't let me alone I have to do something. I wouldn't say my life is worth much, but you know how it is, a guy often puts a sentimental value on staying alive. So those are the symptoms, Doc...

He said aloud, "You're on vacation, Doc. Stay on it, will you? There's nothing wrong with me but too many martinis and late hours and a little too much pressure at work. Thanks anyway."

The other man got up. "Don't mention it, Wayne. But I'll be glad to help any time." He returned to his place near the front of the bus.

Bill closed his eyes and tried to relax, and then felt the seat jarred as a man sat down beside him. He turned and scowled at the guy. Maybe he ought to put up a turnstile and charge admission. The newcomer was a middle-aged character with a square red face and shoulders that crowded him against the side of the bus. He wore a rust-colored sports jacket and yellow sports shirt. Bill had noticed him a couple of times before, pointing out firmly to Holly Clark how arrangements for the trip could be improved.

"Heard you talking to that doctor," the man said. "I'm just two seats ahead so I couldn't help hearing. You did just right, telling him to mind his business."

Bill said, "I get a lot of practice telling people that."

"My name's Blakeslee. George M. Blakeslee. I'm in lumber. No sir, once a man gets in the hands of a pill roller, it's just too bad. Now take me. Never sick a day in my life. You know why? I stay away from doctors."

"When they let me," Bill said, "I stay away from people."

"You don't want to do that. Bad for a man. You ought to mix with people. Trip like this is the best thing in the world for a man. Get out. Meet new people. See new places. Travel gets a man's mind off his troubles."

"This trip's starting to give me new ones," Bill said, wondering if that would register. It didn't, though.

"I admit it isn't arranged perfectly. Not the way I'd handle things if I were running it. But it isn't bad, though. I've been on worse. Last summer the wife and I took a trip through New England and..."

You couldn't handle this guy gently. "Look, Blakeslee," he said bluntly, "I'd like to rest. Do you mind letting me do it?"

"Sure, sure," Blakeslee said. "Know just how you feel. Just thought I'd take a moment to cheer you up. Mark my words, in a few more days you'll be back in the pink and sleeping like a baby." He got up, slapped Bill on the shoulder and left.

This was going to be quite a trip if everybody on the bus had a pet recipe for cheering him up. Probably they all meant well, but he wasn't likely to start sleeping like a baby in the near future. Not while he had an ugly little hunch that one of his pals knew he was on this bus, heading west.

Three

He closed the door of his tourist-court room and pulled the curtains across the windows so nobody could look in. The inside of his mouth tasted like an old inner tube and he could feel his heartbeat down to his toes. He was in Cheyenne, where Russ lived. Big dumb Russ, who might or might not talk. Who might or might not find out whether a guy named Bill Wayne could kill a man if he had to. Big dumb Russ.

Maybe he was overworking that word dumb. Let's pretend Russ was the one who shot him that time in China. Then suppose that, a few weeks ago, somebody in Philadelphia sent Russ a newspaper clipping attached to a note saying, "Didn't you know this guy?" Russ wasn't so dumb he couldn't read. The newspaper clipping would tell him Bill Wayne was alive and back home.

Maybe a brilliant guy would decide in five seconds that Bill Wayne might come around asking awkward questions and looking for trouble. Maybe it would take a brilliant guy all of a few hours to get started for Philadelphia, to head off the trouble before it began. It might take big dumb Russ a couple of days to get to the same point. But he would end up just as dangerous as the brilliant guy.

He unstrapped his suitcase and hauled out the automatic. It was a hunk of metal finished in rattlesnake gray. The thing sat up in his hand alertly, as if it were alive and had a mind of its own. He yanked back the slide and eased it forward and heard the solid *snick* of a cartridge seating itself in the firing chamber. Then he pulled the window curtain aside a few inches and peered out.

Across the way Holly Clark was talking to a couple of members of the Treasure Trip party. He heard her voice clearly. She was saying, "Yes, we're really going to see a rodeo this afternoon. Of course it's too early for the Cheyenne Frontier Days, which is the big rodeo, but one of the ranches near town will put on a riding and roping and shooting exhibition for us. We ought to start by two-thirty."

He let the curtain fall back into place, looked at his watch. It was two o'clock. He wasn't going to the rodeo; he had told Holly he had a headache and wanted to rest. What he actually planned to do was wait until the Treasure Trip party got a good head start, and then scout around town to find out where Russ lived and worked. Meanwhile it might be nice to have the .45 handy. He wasn't forgetting the nights he had lain awake recently, wondering if one of the gang knew he was on the bus heading west.

Hunches were queer things. Especially hunches that somebody was stalking you. Like the doc said that morning on the bus, it might be the result of your subconscious mind adding up tiny facts into a big one.

A guy shot at him and nicked his left side one night last month in Philadelphia. The gunman had to be one of his five former pals. The morning after the shooting he decided to get busy and settle things, and went to New York to shop for a packaged tour that visited the right places. He spent a couple of weeks in New York making his choice. Then he went to Chicago and waited for the tour to start. And all during that time, a hunch that he was being followed had grown stronger and stronger.

It wasn't anything he could nail down. It might be a combination of tiny things: footsteps keeping pace with him too often, a vaguely familiar figure melting into a crowd, travel folders in his hotel room lying in a slightly different pattern than the way he had left them. The weird part of it was that he couldn't imagine Russ or Ken or Frankie or Cappy or Domenic getting away with anything like that. He ought to be able to spot one of them a mile away.

He wasn't going to take any chances, though. He had played target long enough and it was his turn to have the first shot. He stretched out on his bed and slipped the automatic under his pillow. It wouldn't do any harm to relax before his trip into town.

He didn't plan to go to sleep. And when he awoke he was ready to swear he hadn't been sleeping. But a certain fact said he had been. The door was open. He couldn't see the doorway without turning because it

was on a line with the head of the bed. But he could
see an extra splash of light on the rear wall and feel a
faint stirring of air. He remembered he had failed to
lock the door. It hadn't blown open, though. It had a
good latch. A hand had opened it softly and someone
was standing in the doorway.

He moved slowly, like a man stirring in sleep, and
let his right hand slide under the pillow and curl
around the grip of the big automatic. He took a deep
breath, held it, leaped up. A girl was in the doorway.
Not Russ or Cappy or Ken or Frankie or Domenic. A
girl. He had to work it out slowly because his brain
was churning along in a rut and didn't want to leave it.
A girl. Holly Clark.

She stared at the gun in his hand, shrank back.
"Bill!" she gasped. "What's the matter?"

He leaned down and shoved the .45 under the
pillow. His hand was shaking a little. "You don't want
to walk in on me like that," he said. "What's the idea?"

"But I knocked," she said weakly. "I knocked and
called your name. You didn't answer."

"Do you always walk into a guy's room when he
doesn't answer? It must get you some interesting
experiences."

"I'm awfully sorry. I was telling Dr. Brown about
your headache and of course he knows you haven't
been sleeping and I coaxed him to write out a prescription that might help. I came here to give it to you.
When you didn't answer, I scribbled a note and

planned to leave it and the prescription in here."

"I thought you were a big girl now and were going to stop tagging after me."

"I don't consider this tagging after you. It's my job to run the tour, and keep everybody happy and healthy."

"Yeah? Well, I enjoy being miserable."

"Bill, about that gun you grabbed—"

"I always sleep with a gun under my pillow. Habit I picked up in the war."

"I don't believe it. And I'm beginning to wonder about that nervous breakdown you claim you had."

"Is there any way I can coax you to mind your own business?"

"Maybe there is. Will you answer one question honestly? Bill, are you in trouble? Are you running from anything? Is there anything I can do to help?"

"I'm not in trouble. I'm not running from anything. I don't need any help. If that was one question you must be triplets. Now let me ask a question. Are you going to worry about that gun?"

She studied his face earnestly. "I wonder," she said, "if you've changed a lot since the days when I tagged around after you."

"What's that got to do with it?"

"If you haven't changed much, I won't worry."

"You better pick another way to judge me. I'm a different guy."

"I'm not sure," she said. "Well, I have to get the

others to that rodeo. I'll tell you later if I'm worrying."

She walked out of the room. He closed the door and locked it. There was certainly no danger that his former pals would ever blow his brains out, because they wouldn't have anything to aim at. It took real genius for stupidity to leave the door unlocked and fall asleep and then jump up waving the automatic at Holly. For all he knew, she might go running to Doc Brown to ask how you cured homicidal mania.

He went to the window and watched as Holly shepherded the Treasure Trippers into the bus. She seemed fairly calm, and didn't pull Doc Brown aside for a conference, but you couldn't tell what was going on inside her head.

There wasn't anything he could do but go on with his plans, and hope that Holly would decide he was still her football hero. He watched the bus leave, and then dressed for the trip into town. He put on a flowered sports shirt, dark blue slacks and two-toned shoes. He slung a camera on a leather strap over his shoulder. The costume made him officially a tourist, entitled to ask all kinds of questions and poke his nose everywhere without exciting suspicion. He gave the Treasure Trippers a good head start, and walked down the highway into Cheyenne. Nobody paid any attention to him. Now and then he passed tough-looking characters in tight blue jeans and sweaty shirts and broad-brimmed hats, and found that they were inclined to step carefully around him like kids trained not to trample on flower beds. His tourist disguise must be good.

What he wanted to do was check on Russ Nordhoff's address, make sure he was in town, and work out a plan for moving in on him after dark. In case Russ was out of town—and of course he might be—the idea was to case the setup thoroughly. Then he could return to Cheyenne, at some future date, and know what to do without asking questions that would leave a suspicious trail.

At the first drug store he went in and looked up Russ in the phone book. Nordhoff, Russell J. The guy had an auto repairing shop, which seemed logical. Russ had been a good mechanic when you could get him working. He went into a booth and called the number.

"Hello," a voice growled. "Hello."

Good old Russ. Imagine bumping into you here. He said in a high thin voice, "This is Jimmy Smith out to the Bar 4 ranch. I got a car I'd like to sell you, but I can't get in till tonight. Are you gonna be open tonight, or could I maybe bring it around to your house?"

"Cars," Russ said disgustedly. "All guys want to do is sell cars, never buy them. I got used cars coming out my ears."

"I wouldn't want too much for it. I won it off a guy and I already have a car of my own and if I can get a couple hundred out of it that's all I want."

"Bring it around, then. I'll be working here till ten tonight."

Something had happened to good old Russ. The guy must have insomnia. Back in the Air Force what he had was sleeping sickness. "Okay," he said, "I'll be around."

He hung up and left the drug store. This ought to be like shooting fish in a barrel, except that Russ was a little too big to get in the average barrel. It might be a good idea to keep remembering how big Russ was, and that he had once done some fighting in the pro ring. Anybody who wanted to get tough with Russ ought to do it from a greater distance than arm's length.

He checked the address of the garage on his map of Cheyenne and took a walk down that way to make sure he knew the route. It was on a quiet side street east of town, with no houses close. Very convenient. The garage was also within half a mile of the tourist court on U.S. 30 where the Treasure Trip party was staying overnight. Russ couldn't have chosen the place more thoughtfully.

After returning to the tourist court, he sat around feeding half-smoked cigarettes into ashtrays, waiting for the Treasure Trip bus to return. It was nearly six o'clock when he heard it easing to a halt with a tired sigh from its air brakes. He went out to see if there were any signs that Holly had been babbling about the gun to Doc Brown.

First off the bus were Mrs. Craig, Mrs. Anders, Mrs. Cooper and Mrs. Allingham. They were plump middle-aged women who always called each other girls, maybe in the hope that somebody would think they were. Ordinarily he tried to avoid them but now he couldn't. They closed in on him with squeaks of pleasure and began telling him how much he had missed by not going to the rodeo. The show at the ranch had left them breathless; you might think that a cowboy had tried to fling each of them over his saddle and ride away into the sunset. Other people getting off the bus seemed to be excited, too. Mr. Jorgenson— hardware, Peoria—was telling Mrs. Jorgenson with rare firmness that he thought he would have three fingers of whiskey before dinner, and for once Mrs. Jorgenson wasn't telling him to remember his stomach. Clara Oakes, the thin girl of about twenty who usually followed her mother like a new calf, had turned maverick and was giggling with the bus driver.

He kept looking for Holly. She hadn't got off the bus yet.

Mrs. Craig and Mrs. Anders and Mrs. Cooper and Mrs. Allingham kept chattering at him. The reason for all the excitement, he gathered, was a handsome cowboy who had been in the rodeo staged by the ranch. Compared to him, other cowboys were not quite fit to ride on a merry-go-round. After the rodeo the handsome cowboy had apparently talked man-to-woman with Mrs. Craig, Mrs. Anders, Mrs. Cooper and Mrs. Allingham, and had talked man-to-man with Mr. Jorgenson, and had talked boy-to-girl with Clara

Oakes. He was very tall and had floppy yellow hair and either blue eyes or gray eyes, according to whether you believed Mrs. Anders or Mrs. Cooper.

Doc Brown got off the bus with Mrs. Brown, waved cheerfully at him and called, "Great show, Wayne. Should have been there." That sounded innocent enough. The guy wouldn't have been so casual if Holly had told him about the gun.

George M. Blakeslee climbed out, telling everybody that it had been pretty fair, for a strictly amateur rodeo, but that it didn't touch the real professional rodeos. Although, of course, everybody knew that in the big rodeos the riders arranged in advance who was to win.

That emptied the bus and Holly hadn't appeared. He broke in on something Mrs. Allingham was saying, and asked, "Where's Miss Clark?"

"She was a naughty girl," Mrs. Anders said playfully. "She stole our cowboy. Didn't she, girls?"

"Indeed she did," Mrs. Cooper trilled. "She's back there in his car."

He looked where Mrs. Cooper was pointing, and saw a convertible with the top down parked behind the bus. Holly Clark was in it. She was talking gaily to the driver, who wore a big white Stetson slanting back on his floppy yellow hair. That would be the champion cowboy.

"What do you think of *that?*" Mrs. Allingham asked breathlessly.

He thought it was a pretty good idea. While Holly was playing with her cowboy, she wouldn't have the time or desire to worry about the problems of Bill Wayne. He said, "She's been working hard running this tour. Glad to see her having a little fun."

Mrs. Cooper said, "It would be nicer if he rode around on a horse instead of in a car. But I suppose he needs a car. After all, being a deputy sheriff—"

"A what?" Bill said sharply.

"He's a deputy sheriff."

A chill skated over him. "I thought you said he was a cowboy."

"Oh no! He's a deputy sheriff. He just happened to be at that ranch and he wanted to make sure we saw a good show and he was wonderful, just wonderful."

He didn't go for this. Holly had talked about his health with a doctor. Maybe she wanted to talk about his .45 with a deputy sheriff. He'd better try to break up this little party, if things hadn't gone too far already. "I think I'd like to meet him," he said, and walked toward the convertible. Holly didn't see him coming because she was chatting too happily. He paused beside the car and said, "Sorry to interrupt, but is this one of the nights when we pay for our own dinners?"

Holly gave a guilty jump, turned to him. "Oh, it's Bill," she said. "Why…why yes, it is. Treasure Trip only pays for meals when we're staying at American Plan hotels."

"Thanks," he said, without making a move to leave.

She waited a moment, then said in an embarrassed way, "Bill, this is Carson Smith. Deputy Sheriff Smith. Carson, this is Bill Wayne."

The big man behind the wheel flipped a hand casually. "Howdy, Wayne," he said. He had a drawling voice with guitar tones in it.

That sounded casual enough, Bill thought. Not as if Smith had been told anything about the .45. Smith hadn't looked at him with special interest, either. "Hi," he said. Now the idea was to get Holly away from the guy and eliminate any chance that she might talk about the gun.

"Bill is one of our party," Holly said. "But he had a headache and stayed here to rest this afternoon."

"I hope you done got over that headache," Smith said. "Had a headache once myself, account of a bronc kicking me in the head. Warn't no fun, neither. Sorry you had to miss our show."

Maybe the guy had talked man-to-man with Mr. Jorgenson, but now he gave the impression that he was talking man-to-boy. It was annoying. It was going to be a pleasure to mess up the guy's play for Holly. "From what people tell me," he said, "your show was the most exciting thing that's happened out west since Custer's last stand. But I got the impression that if you had been at the Little Big Horn, it would have been Sitting Bull's last stand."

Smith gave a pleased chuckle. "Why, thank you, pardner. Glad the folks liked it."

What did you have to use to get through this character's hide—spurs? Let's try again, Wayne. "They said when you rode you were just like a part of the horse. Which part would that have been?"

"Bill!" Holly said. Then she turned to Smith and explained, "He's just making a joke. Don't mind him."

Carson Smith considered that idea as if sizing up a spavined cowpony. "Only thing is," he said, "a joke had ought to be funny, hadn't it?"

There was an awkward pause, and Holly said, "Did you have a nice rest this afternoon, Bill?"

"Yes, thanks."

Another pause. They were waiting for him to go away, but he wasn't planning to. Holly said rather desperately, "Would you like to know a good place to have dinner? Carson has been telling me about some good places."

"Fine," Bill said. "And by the way, I was hoping you might have dinner with me." He didn't want to take her to dinner, and it might be awkward to get rid of her afterward, but it was one way to block out Smith.

She looked startled. "I'm afraid I couldn't," she said. "You see, I…" She paused, looked hopefully at Smith.

Bill frowned. It wasn't nice to see a girl fish so openly for an invitation. He said smoothly and quickly, before Smith could take the hook, "Of course. I forgot you have to take care of the whole party of us. Selfish of me. She's a very dutiful girl about her work, Smith. Never lets anything interfere."

Holly looked at him as if he were coiled in the dust making rattling noises.

Carson Smith blinked his eyes—blue, by the way, as Mrs. Anders had claimed—and rumbled, "Well, I reckon I better say goodbye then, ma'am. Been mighty nice." He got out his side of the car and spent a few seconds rising to his full height. Probably he wasn't over six feet four, however, if you didn't count six inches of hat and two inches of high-heeled boots. Everything about the guy was king-size including the revolver in a hand-tooled holster on his hip. He came around the car and helped Holly out and tipped his hat and said goodbye and drove away.

"Well!" Holly said furiously. "That was a lovely performance you put on. Like a Russian at a peace conference. Did you have some reason to interfere?"

"I thought you were neglecting your job. Aren't you supposed to take care of the rest of us?"

"You certainly haven't wanted me to do anything for you. As for the rest of them, I'm not on call every minute. Carson asked if he could drive me back and I saw no reason why I shouldn't accept. For a change it was nice to talk to a man with charming manners."

"I wasn't very charmed. The moment he heard about my headache, he had to brag that it took a kick from a horse to give him one."

"You deliberately went out of your way to get rid of him. He was going to ask me to dinner."

"Probably I saved you from baked beans around a campfire."

"Oh, I don't understand you at all!" she cried. "First you don't want to have anything to do with me, and now you come around interfering. I would have had a wonderful evening with Carson if you hadn't spoiled things."

"I must say he stampeded easily. I don't think he would even have worked up to holding your hand. Well, all this talk about dinner has made me hungry. Believe I'll run along."

"You'll run along?" she said indignantly. "You can't do that. You just cheated me out of a nice dinner. A gentleman would try to make it up to me."

He grinned. "If you're hinting for another dinner invitation from me, no sale. But I will do something for you. If I see a gentleman around, I'll tell him to look you up."

He turned and walked away. She was quite a girl. If she didn't have so many bad qualities, and if he didn't have some personal business in Cheyenne, it might have been fun to take her to dinner.

He located a quiet restaurant in Cheyenne and ordered dinner and then found that he wasn't hungry. All he could think of was the fact that he had to move in on Russ in a few hours. He would stand there with the .45 in his hand and tell Russ to come clean and maybe Russ would balk and then he would have to find out if he could put a slug through the guy. Other men in the war had been luckier. They had been taught how to kill. All the Air Corps had taught him was how to take up a transport plane and bring it down in one piece.

After leaving the restaurant he went back to the tourist court and slipped into his room and got out the .45. He removed the clip and shucked out the bullets and wiped them to remove any excess grease. The bullets were big ugly things and he didn't like the feel of them in his hand. However, he hadn't liked the feel of the one that had ripped into his back, either.

He stayed in his room with the light off. Sunset flared in the west like the fires of an Indian massacre. He waited until the light faded, then put on a sports jacket, buttoned it, and went out trying to look like a man with a heavy dinner rather than a .45 automatic under his belt. Nobody was around, but just to be on the safe side he walked toward the center of town before cutting away from U.S. 30 and heading for the garage.

As he walked, his imagination started to give him a bad time. The window curtains of houses seemed to quiver as if people were spying on him. A cottonwood tree dangled a dead branch against the sky like a gallows. Odd rustlings trailed him down the street and halted abruptly when he jerked his head around to see what was causing them. By the time he reached the garage his heart felt ready for a carbon and valve job. He walked past the place several times on the far side of the street, studying the setup. Lights were on in the repair shop and the overhead doors were up. Off in one corner a big guy in coveralls was working at a bench. It was like old times to see Russ in coveralls standing at a bench, except for the fact that Russ was working. Back in the old days he would just have been standing.

Nobody else was in sight, and the nearest house was a block away. He got out the automatic and jacked a cartridge into the chamber. Then he walked across the street and into the shop. Russ didn't realize he had a visitor, because his back was turned and he was using a power tool that made a high spitting whine.

The guy's back looked like a wonderful target. His own back must have looked that way just before the slug tore into it in China. Maybe he ought to think about drilling Russ right now, while his back was turned, while the power tool was making such a racket. He had a hunch that Russ wasn't going to talk. So plugging him now would save trouble. Why was it worse to shoot a man in the back than in the front? The result was the same. In fact it was probably the humane thing to do because it was all over before the guy knew what hit him. Lots of guys had been shot in the back and hadn't objected to it.

He looked at the automatic and at Russ's back. His

stomach began feeling as if he were pulling out of a steep dive. It was no use arguing with himself. He hadn't been brought up in a tough enough school. He was trained to pat a guy on the back, not to put a bullet in it.

Four

He reached out disgustedly and flipped the switch that controlled the overhead doors. They came clanking and rumbling down behind him. Russ turned. He stood there like a big startled grizzly, mouth open, eyes staring, long arms dangling, rolling his head slowly from side to side and sniffing as if to get the scent.

"Bill," he said. "Jeez, it's Bill."

"I'll take it from there. The next line is, jeez, Bill, I thought you was dead."

"Jeez, no, I didn't. Some guy I knew in Philly sends me a story out of the paper saying you was alive and back home and I figure papers can't make up stuff like that and—Bill, old guy, it's good to see you!"

He came shambling forward, wiping his right hand on the coveralls and then holding it out in front of him like a man groping through a dark room. A smile oozed onto his face and froze there. It made him look as happy as if he had broken a leg and a doctor was starting to set it.

Bill lifted the automatic and said softly, "You want to shake hands with this?"

Russ stopped as if he had walked into a wall. He

stared at the weapon and muttered, "That's a gun."

"Wonderful what Air Force training will do for a man. Yeah, you guessed it. It's not a bunch of posies but a forty-five-caliber Government Model Colt Automatic Pistol."

"Whatcha doing with a gun, Bill?"

"I'm carrying it in my right hand, Russ. You know what? It's legal to tote a gun in Wyoming as long as it isn't concealed. I don't know whether it's also legal to shoot a guy with an unconcealed gun but maybe I'll find out."

Russ's face was grimy and the sweat coming out on it looked like drippings from a crankcase. He said hoarsely, "You don't want to shoot me, Bill."

"That's odd. I thought I did. How do you suppose I got the idea?"

"Jeez, well, maybe you had some screwy idea I was the guy plugged you back in Nanking. Don't get sore, now. I'm not saying you're screwy. I guess it's a natural thing, a guy has a dust-up with his friends and starts walking away and bingo, he's shot."

"You mean it's a natural thing that, bingo, I was shot?"

Russ wiped a sleeve across his eyes and left a white mask around them. "No, I mean it's a natural thing that...that...now I forget what I meant. You know. Help a guy out, will you?"

"It's a natural thing to figure you shot me?"

"You got me wrong, Bill! I wasn't even there! I was

going out the back door of the office and you was walking out the front and one of these dumb Nationalist soldiers was excited and didn't know the score and told you to halt and you didn't hear and he upped with his rifle and plugged you."

"You saw all that through the building?"

"They tell me about it afterward, Bill. And we all think you're dead and we go after this dumb soldier and—"

"He couldn't have been dumb, Russ. Anybody who can shoot a forty-five pistol bullet out of an Army rifle is pretty clever."

"Was it a forty-five? Yeah, that's right, he plugs you with a forty-five automatic and we all run out of the office—"

"How did you get back in the office so fast? You'd gone out the back, remember?"

"You keep mixing a guy up!"

"No, I keep trying to untangle you. Okay, so my old pal Russ got to me first and—were you first, Russ?"

"I, uh, maybe I was second or third. So we got to where you was lying. So we got there, see? Then, uh, then…"

"It's tough to work this part out, isn't it, Russ? Because nobody carried me back into the office or cut open my shirt or broke out a first-aid kit or anything. You just let me lie there on my face and beat it the hell out to the plane and took off."

Russ gulped. It looked as though he might be trying to swallow a piston. "Yeah," he mumbled, "it don't look good. Only you got to remember the whole joint was in a flap and it looked like you was dead. But you know I never shot you, Bill. We always got along good. I'm your pal, see? Ask me right now and you can have the shirt off my back."

"Maybe I'll wait until it has a bullet hole in it."

Russ said in a cracked whisper, "You got the wrong guy. Maybe one of the others did plug you. Honest, like I said I went out the back and all I know is what they told me and things was so mixed up a guy had no time to check. Go see the other guys, Bill. You know where to find them?"

"Sure. You all wrote very sad letters to my folks, after you got back, about how I'd been captured by the Reds. And you've all been swell guys and have been sending my folks Christmas cards ever since. So my addresses are pretty good. Your last Christmas card was so pretty I hate to think of shooting you."

"Look, Bill. You shoot me and get caught and then you'll never find out if one of the others done it."

"What makes you think I'll get caught if I shoot you?"

"Jeez, Bill, everybody'll know you done it."

"Nobody knows I'm here except you. I've never told anybody what really happened to me back in Nanking. It would only have worried my folks. And as for telling the cops, hell, what could I prove? I figured that would put me in the middle when I started to settle things myself. No, Russ. There isn't a cop in the world who'll have any reason to suspect me if you get found shot up."

"The others will know. Cappy and Domenic and Ken and Frankie."

"Maybe they won't hear about what happened to you before I drop in to tell them."

Russ backed away a few steps. He licked his lips with a gray tongue, glanced at the workbench beside him. He seemed to study the position of a tire iron lying on the bench. His right hand, close to the tire iron, twitched.

Bill said, "I'm following right along, chum. Yeah, that works both ways, doesn't it? If nobody knows why I'm here and if you get a chance to knock me off and drop me out in some gully, you're in the clear. But if I were you I wouldn't bet a tire iron against a forty-five."

The big hand near the tire iron stopped twitching and began to shake. "There's a guy coming to see me," Russ said. "He might be here any sec. Maybe he's right outside listening. So you couldn't get away with it, see? He'd put the cops onto you."

"A guy named Jimmy Smith?" Bill asked gently. "From the Bar 4 ranch?"

"Yeah! That's the guy. It's the straight dope. He wants to sell me a car. You don't have to believe me but—"

"He won it off a guy and you can have it for a couple hundred bucks."

"Yeah, that's it, and he'll be here any second and...and—" An idea hit him like a punch in the stomach. After a moment he said faintly, "You was the guy that called."

"Uh-huh. So I don't think we'll be disturbed."

"Now look, Bill, don't be hasty. Let's talk this over. I'm getting an idea."

"What kind of an idea?"

"Give me a couple seconds, will you? I got to wrassle with it."

Russ was wrestling with an idea, all right, and there seemed to be some question who would win. That didn't necessarily mean it was a big idea. Sometimes even a little one could throw Russ. This one seemed to be rocking him with forearm blows and body slams. Russ was looking as pained as a wrestler in a television bout, except that in this case the match was on the level.

"Hurry up," Bill said. "I can't wait all night. I have a date with an alibi."

"Now look," Russ said with a great effort, "how about if I tell you how you can cut yourself a nice hunk of change? Maybe a quarter million bucks. Only you got to be sensible about this shooting business."

"First let's be sensible about the quarter million. That's a lot of money to talk about. You don't look like you have a speaking acquaintance with more than a couple hundred."

"Yeah? Well, I got a speaking acquaintance with half a million bucks. In gold, too."

"Sure. You have an ancient map to the Lost Dutchman Mine or Montezuma's treasure. An old prospector gave it to you on his deathbed. We look for a mountain that throws the shadow of a skull on a valley just as the full moon comes up in August."

"The map I have," Russ said doggedly, "is a nice modern oil company road map. And we don't look for no mountains. We look for a C-47 plane that crashed."

"This is getting to be quite a yarn. Is this supposed to be our C-47 you're talking about?"

"Don't be like that, Bill. I'm leveling with you. Sure, it's our C-47. It was carrying half a million bucks in gold. The stuff was in boxes marked with Chinese writing saying they held medical supplies. You sure ought to remember them boxes. Don't you?"

Russ could no more make up a yarn like this than he could do a toe dance in the ballet. "Yes," Bill said thoughtfully, "I remember those boxes. I wanted them thrown off the plane. I begin to see why everybody got so upset."

"I said we ought to tell you what was in them boxes. But no, the other guys said it wouldn't make no difference to you. So bingo, there's got to be a shooting."

"You're giving up that yarn about the soldier potting me by mistake, are you?"

"All right. You're too smart to buy that. But it still wasn't me that did it."

"Who did?"

Russ set his jaw stubbornly. "I don't know. You want to talk about this dough or don't you?"

"Okay, Russ. What happened to the Chinese black market guy who owned those boxes?"

"Oh, him? You know how the starboard door on that plane didn't latch good? We hit an air pocket and that door flipped open and he fell out. He was standing too close to it."

"He was standing too close to one of you guys."

"I wouldn't know," Russ said, without interest. "I was up on the flight deck at the time."

"Natch. Then what happened?"

"Well, we come in to Hong Kong and we figure we better not try cashing in the gold there. So we headed Stateside by way of the Philippines and Japan and the Aleutians and Alaska and Canada. That's when things went wrong. We didn't know if some customs guy in the U.S. might get nosy about them boxes so we figured on not landing at any regular field. We figured on setting down way out in the Bonneville Salt Flats in Utah and hiding the boxes. Only what with trying not to make too many stops we stretched the gas too far. So there we are with the tanks running dry and nothing under us but a lot of lousy mountaintops."

"With guys like you I don't know how we ever flew the Hump."

"You should talk!" Russ cried. "All right, so if you had been running things it wouldn't have happened.

And why weren't you running things? Because you'd turned chaplain on us. So who was dumb first?"

"I won't argue. I was dumb first. What did you do when you ran out of gas? Bail out?"

"With all that dough aboard? Jeez, we'd have ridden it down right into a mountain. But Ken spotted a lake. He ditched the plane on the lake right nice. But all we had time to do was break out a rubber raft and shove off before she sank. So all that dough is just waiting there to be brought up."

"That was a long time ago. I'd have expected you guys to grow fins and gills diving for it."

"All right, wise guy. There's a hundred feet of water over the plane."

"That's nothing for a trained diver in a suit. None of you felt like learning?"

"Sure, we felt like learning. Cappy and Domenic out on the coast have both learned. Trouble is, that ain't no deserted lake. It has a dozen cabins where guys come up for vacations and weekends. Any time the roads are open so we could truck in a good-sized boat and an air pump and diving suits, somebody's there fishing or lying around. It's not a big lake. Anybody on shore can see most of it. We don't dare go after that stuff with people watching. An hour after we started diving, we'd have to shoot some curious dope."

"Times have changed. Now nobody wants to shoot anybody."

"Who likes to shoot people?" Russ said in a hurt

voice. "There's another way to handle it. We been buying up the lousy lake. We got all the land now except around six of the cabins. A couple years more and we can afford to buy those. Then we block off the road and go to work. It's taken a lot of dough and we sure been sweating to earn it."

This was good. You could call it poetic justice. The five of them started out to make a fast buck and ended by earning slow pennies. Sometimes fate showed a nice sense of humor. "You mentioned me getting a quarter million bucks," he said. "With six guys cutting into half a million, how does one come out with a quarter million? Did the five of you talk it over and decide you'd better pay me off big?"

"We ain't talked it over."

"Well then, what happened when you told them about that newspaper clipping saying I was back?"

"I didn't tell them you was back."

"That's queer. Why not?"

Russ looked embarrassed. "I figgered maybe you'd want to surprise them. How did I know you would drop in on me first?"

"Was that friendly? I might have hurt one of them."

"Let 'em get hurt," Russ said bitterly. "Crashing that plane because they couldn't figure the fuel right! Taking it easy while I sweat my eyes out here! I been putting in more toward buying that lousy lake than any two of them. I ain't had a day off from this joint in two years."

"What about that little trip you took to Philadelphia last month? Didn't that count as time off?"

Russ peered out from under heavy eyebrows as if his eyes were small wary animals. "I didn't take no trip."

"Somebody took a shot at me last month in Philadelphia."

"One of the others did, then. I was here. I can prove it."

"But if they didn't know I was back and you did—"

"Maybe somebody sent them a clipping too!" Russ cried. "All I know is I was here and you can ask anybody."

The guy seemed to mean it. "We haven't settled this angle of how I rate half the money, with five others cutting in."

"Who said anything about five others?"

"Oh."

"After all," Russ said, "one of the others shot you. If you only knocked off one of them you might not get the right guy. So after you finish making sure you got the right guy, that leaves me and you."

"Or if I wasn't careful it might leave just you."

"What a nasty mind you got," Russ said virtuously.

He wasn't doing very well at making Russ say who shot him. Maybe if he could find out where the lake was, he could make Russ talk by threatening to spill everything to the customs authorities. And if Russ still wouldn't talk, the same threat might make one of the others come across. He said casually, "Where is this lake, Russ?"

"I'm holding that out for a while. It's all I have to sell, and you ain't made no offer."

"What would you consider a fair offer?"

"You got something on me but I don't have anything on you. When I hear that Frankie or Domenic or Cappy or Ken has been knocked off, that will give me something on you. Then I'll tell you where the lake is."

His hand tightened on the .45. "I'll make you an offer. Either give me your map of that lake, or I'll give you thirty seconds to live."

Russ seemed to shrink inside the coveralls. His left shoulder hunched forward: a ring-wise fighter covering his jaw. "And after I give you the map," he said thickly, "you'll give me one second to live."

"You just wasted eight seconds. Give me the map and you're okay."

"Why should I trust you?"

"Because you don't have a better choice. Call it a gamble if you want. Maybe you'll lose. But you'll lose anyway if you don't gamble. You'd better not let me talk because it's running out the clock on you. Now we only have ten seconds to go."

"I wasn't the guy shot you."

"It's been nice knowing you."

"You're kicking away a quarter million bucks."

"Five…four…three…"

Russ took a deep breath "Two, one, out," he said.

He aimed at the third button from the top of the coveralls and took up the trigger slack and squeezed slowly and waited for the crash and the upward flip of the muzzle. It seemed to take a long time.

Russ said hoarsely, "I'm betting you won't shoot."

He glanced down. It wasn't the fault of the safety catch. The thing was all ready to shoot. He felt sweat coming out on his body like heat rash. He squeezed again. Nothing happened.

Russ said, "I'm betting you *can't* shoot."

He looked down at his hand. Muscles twitched in it and tendons made white streaks against the skin, but nothing happened. There was a short circuit some-where in the nerves between his head and hand. When he told his hand to squeeze the trigger it went into a deep freeze, without budging. The frozen feeling crept up his arm and into his body and left a chunk of ice in his stomach.

"All right, Russ," he muttered. "You've got a good bet."

He felt suddenly very weak and silly. His right hand started to ache, as if it had been in a numbing vise. "You wouldn't care to make a sudden move and help me out?"

"Listen, pal, after a gamble like that, the only move I want to make is to lie down."

"What gave you the idea, Russ?"

"Aah, you always did have a lot of chaplain in you. Then you talked too much. Guys who shoot off their mouths don't shoot off many guns. Why don't you put that thing away now?"

"I'll keep it handy. I might find myself at a loss for words."

"Here's a hot tip for you, kid. Don't go walking in on Ken or Cappy or Domenic waving a rod you ain't gonna use. You'll end up catching a shovelful of dirt in your face."

This was great. You come two thousand miles to make a guy talk or to shoot him, and lose your nerve and then let him tell you to be a good boy and to quit playing with dangerous things like loaded guns. What did you do now? Thank him humbly and walk out? Lacking any better ideas, it looked as if you did.

He snapped on the safety catch of the .45 and started turning toward the door.

His move set off a chain reaction. As he began turning, his eyes flashed a series of action photos to his brain: Russ grabbing a tire iron…lifting the thing… throwing it. The action came fast but his brain was right in there catching it all and telling him exactly how to duck and wheel and flick off the safety and let Russ have a slug. His brain did a real jet-propelled job. Unfortunately his body was heavy with inertia and kept turning away from Russ the whole time this was going on. Trying to change its course was like wrestling with a car skidding on ice.

A dull shock exploded up his right arm. The tire iron caromed off and went clanging over concrete.

The .45 dropped to the floor. Now that it was much too late his body came out of the skid. He wheeled, saw Russ charging in. There was no time to throw a punch. He ducked under the blurred streaks of heavy fists, lunged forward. It was like being a kid again and catching the tackling dummy with a solid shoulder block. Russ folded across his shoulder like a sack of sand. He tried to keep his feet moving, to keep charging and slam Russ into a wall or bench or car. It didn't work. His shoes couldn't dig into concrete the way cleats would dig into turf. He slipped and lost power and felt Russ starting to claw at his body. That was no good. In another second Russ would have his breath back and begin making a pretzel out of him.

He jerked aside suddenly. Russ tottered forward, off balance. They invented right hooks for times like this. He aimed one at the guy's jaw. Nothing happened. His right arm didn't move. It hung at his side, numbed by the blow of the tire iron. Sorry, bud. Our right hooks are out of stock at the moment. He switched and hooked a left. Too late again. Russ was balanced once more, brushed it aside, moved in behind a sawmill whirl of rights and lefts.

He danced back from the blows, jabbing with his left. It was pretty futile. The dam was breaking and he was trying to hold it back with his little finger. The heavy swings began surging over his guard and breaking like surf on his head and body. This wouldn't last long. The big fists didn't hurt but he could feel each one packing him away more snugly into soft black wool.

His foot hit something that clattered and he caught a bleary glimpse of the .45 skittering across the floor. He dived at it. The floor smacked him harder than Russ had done but he got the gun in his left hand and clawed at the safety catch and then a skyrocket went soaring up inside his head and burst and faded in darkness.

Five

It wasn't easy to open his eyes. His eyelids were heavy and he had to jack them up slowly as if he were raising a car wheel to change a tire. Now and then the jack slipped and the eyelids slammed down and he had to start all over again. Finally he got them up so they stayed. It was queer that he had been thinking in terms of jacks and tires because he seemed to be lying on the floor of an auto repair shop.

A few feet away was a car, and beside it a mechanic was lying on his back, probably getting ready to slide under the car on one of those low-wheeled platforms that mechanics use.

He called thickly, "Hey, Mac."

The mechanic didn't hear him. Didn't move, either. Mechanics probably caught up on their sleep when they rolled under cars but this guy didn't even bother to get under the car first. He didn't even mind lying right in a little pool of oil.

If anybody was going to move it looked as if Bill Wayne was elected. It would be nice if that tow truck in the corner would back up to him and drop its hook and crank him up to his feet, but in this joint they only worried about auto bodies, not human ones. He got up slowly. While he was doing it the knocking in his head quickened until he thought a bearing was going to burn out, but once he was up it quit chattering so loudly. His right arm wasn't really crumpled, either. Just numb and asleep.

What a sloppy joint this was. A mechanic sleeping on the floor in a pool of oil, nobody working, tools scattered around. Right at his feet somebody had left a small power tool that looked as if it might be used to drill holes in metal. He stooped, picked it up. That was odd. You didn't use this to drill holes in metal. You used it to drill holes in people. It was a .45 Government Model Colt Automatic Pistol. He sniffed at the muzzle and got an acrid smell that knifed into his head like ammonia and started it clearing.

The pistol had recently been used to drill a hole in somebody. It had done an efficient job. The mechanic lying on the floor was Russ, and that wasn't oil leaking out of his coveralls. That is, not unless they were making oil in dull red shades this season. Russ wasn't getting ready to slide under the car, either; he had no further use for cars, except maybe a hearse.

He looked at his wristwatch and saw that it was a little after ten. He must have been unconscious for almost twenty minutes. Probably Russ had banged his head against the floor or kicked him just as the .45 let go. He tried to picture the way it had happened. There was Russ leaning down to bang his head on the floor. Or there was Russ getting in the kick, poised right over him. And yet Russ had ended on his back eight feet away. A slug from a .45 packed an awful wallop but you wouldn't think it would throw a man around like that. Of course Russ might have staggered backward—not that guys did much staggering when a .45 nailed them in the heart.

That had been quite a shot. It must have been left-handed, too, because his right hand hadn't been in working order. He couldn't have done as well right-handed if he had emptied the whole clip into Russ. He took out the clip and counted the bullets. Five. He worked the slide and ejected the sixth cartridge from the chamber. He picked it up from the floor and, while he was at it, hunted around for the cartridge case of the bullet that had been fired. It had rolled somewhere out of sight and he couldn't find it. He replaced the sixth bullet and shoved the clip back into place. Just out of curiosity he held the automatic in his left hand and practiced aiming it. The thing wobbled as if he were using a popcorn shaker. That left-handed shot of his certainly rated as beginner's luck.

For a moment he was almost tempted to believe he couldn't have done the shooting. But that was just kidding himself, of course. Nobody else had been around who might have done the job. He'd better get out of here fast, if he didn't want to find himself on a witness stand pulling that old gag about everything going black.

The thing to do was not leave many clues. Clue number one was the bullet. They could have it. Clue number two was the cartridge case. Ditto. Clue number three was the switch controlling the garage doors, which he had touched when he arrived. They couldn't have that one; anybody who had been in the Armed Forces had a full set of fingerprints on file in Washington. He went to the switch and wiped it with a handkerchief. Clue number four, footprints. Just to be a good guy he would leave the footprints, seeing that he couldn't mop up the whole floor.

Clue number five was his appearance. He was taking that with him, although not many people would think it was worth the trouble. His clothes were dusty and rumpled, and his body felt as if people had been holding a rodeo on it. He stumbled across the shop and found a washroom. He yanked out a paper towel and cleaned smears of blood and dirt from his face. That uncovered bruises; his face looked like an apple left too long at the bottom of a barrel. He brushed dirt from his clothes and noted that fortunately he hadn't picked up any oil or grease stains. He combed his hair, wiped possible fingerprints from the faucets, switched out the light.

The idea of rolling up the noisy overhead doors didn't appeal to him, and he headed out through the small office beside the shop. He paused a moment to open desk drawers, using a handkerchief, in the hope of finding a map showing the lake where the C-47 had ditched. No maps. He opened the office door, saw the street was empty and walked out.

Sometime in the near future people were going to look at his bruised face and say, "Why, Mr. Wayne, whatever happened to you!" And if, when people asked that question, they had been reading in the paper about a terrific fight in which a man was finally shot and killed, they might connect the two things. He couldn't afford to be connected in any way with Russ because it would be too easy to dig up a motive.

He walked back to U.S. 30. Halfway between the tourist court and town was a scrubby little park. He hid the .45 at the base of a tree and started into town to shop for an alibi. There was a nip in the air and he began buttoning his sports jacket. He fumbled with the second buttonhole and couldn't find the button. He stopped, examined it. The second button was gone. He remembered buttoning the jacket in the evening to hide the .45 tucked under his belt. Quite likely the button had ripped off during the fight, and was lying on the floor of the garage where a cop would find it. He took out a penknife and cut off the other two buttons and threw them away.

He walked into downtown Cheyenne. It was Saturday night and the place was getting ready to kick up its heels. Ranch hands and guys from a nearby military post were prospecting around for excitement. A couple of police cars were riding herd on things, and pairs of MPs moved along the sidewalks peering into bars and taprooms. It looked as if Cheyenne could be a tough town on Saturday night. That was fine; he wanted to pick a fight and collect a few honest lumps and coax the cops to rescue him.

On a side street he found just the kind of taproom he needed; dim lighting that wouldn't call attention to his bruised face, and a rugged-looking crowd at the bar. He marched in, wedged his shoulder between a couple of big cowboys, rammed through to the bar. "Give a guy room, will you?" he snarled. The two ranch hands turned toward him. They were tall rangy guys, and once they started working on him they would probably be about as easy to stop as a stampede. He forced himself to say in a nasty tone, "Who do you think you're staring at?"

The big guy on his right studied him for a moment, then smiled and said, "I'm lookin' at a man that seems to want a drink bad. Don't mind me. Step right in and get one." He called to his friend on the other side, "Ain't that right, Joe?"

"It sure is," the other said. "I'll even buy the man a drink. What'll it be, pardner?"

He looked up at the two big friendly faces and knew he couldn't pick a fight with guys as nice as these. "A shot of rye," he said weakly.

They draped arms as heavy as fence posts over his shoulders and ordered the drink and tossed theirs down and then shook hands and said they had a poker game coming up and had to get back to it. They sauntered out. Great. Everybody loved him. What did you have to do in this town to start a fight? He ordered another drink and lifted it and felt somebody jostle his arm. He swung around fiercely and saw an Army sergeant, the kind of guy who picks his teeth with a bayonet.

"You shoved me, you big ape," he snapped.

The sergeant swung his head around slowly, like a tank turret. After a long moment he said, "Sorry, mister."

What was the Army coming to? "You spilled my drink too."

"All right, mister. I'll buy you another."

"You act tough until somebody gets tough with you, huh?"

The sergeant pulled out a dollar bill and threw it on the counter. "Buy yourself a drink or tear it up," he said crisply. "If you're looking for a fight you have the wrong guy. This town's lousy with MPs. Smacking you down ain't worth these stripes." He wheeled and marched out of the place.

There was too much law and order around Cheyenne: deputy sheriffs, cops in prowl cars, MPs. If any of them were really on the ball they'd be digging up a murder instead of making sure nobody got a black eye. They—

Somebody tapped him on the shoulder. He turned and saw it was the bartender. The guy had a close-cropped cannonball head, and arms like a couple of beer kegs placed on end.

"Out," the bartender said. "You been looking for trouble ever since you got here. Out."

This was one of your real old-time bartenders who could shake up tough drunks faster than he could mix a martini. He leaned across the bar with his face in easy range of the bartender's fists and smiled quietly and said, "Who's going to put me out? You?"

The bartender picked up a phone. "Not me, Mac. We have cops to handle bullies like you...hello, sergeant? Eddy the bartender at the Lone Rider Bar. We got a drunk here looking for a fight and—"

Bill headed for the exit. In a couple more minutes the cops would be swarming around looking for him and he would have no alibi to explain his appearance. The cops wouldn't worry about that at the time, but when they found Russ had been shot after a brawl they might want to ask who he had been fighting. He hurried out through the doorway and crashed into somebody headed the other way.

A thin voice rasped at him, "Whyn't you look where you're going, you big ox! You want a smack in the nose?"

This guy was an Army private. Not a Pfc, just a plain buck private. He was small but he looked angry, and that was the main thing. "Yes," Bill said hopefully. "I want a smack in the nose."

The private swayed slightly. "Okay. Step outside."

"We are outside."

"Yeah?" The private peered around slowly and suspiciously. "Oh," he said, "I get it. You want to start something right in front of this joint so when you get licked your pals can run out and jump me."

"I wouldn't pull a trick like that," Bill said soothingly. "Look. There's an alley right next to us. We can step in there and settle things." He could let the fight start in the alley and take a few punches and come staggering back onto the pavement where everybody could see him getting hit.

The private turned and started for the alley, placing his feet as if afraid he might mislay one. Bill caught up to him and linked an arm through one of his and helped him walk into the alley. Then he stepped back and waited.

"Say," the private said. "You're a pretty good guy, giving me a hand. Maybe I won't put the slug on you after all."

They couldn't do this to him. "Scared, are you?" he snarled.

"Nah. I'm starting to like you. Let's have a drink, huh?"

"I never make friends with a guy until I know he's a real man. You want to make friends with me, you got to fight me."

The little private drew back his right fist. "You asked for it," he said.

He brought the fist around in a wild swing. The alley was dark and Bill couldn't judge where the fist was going. He tried to step into it but the swing looped around his neck and the small soldier lurched forward against him and sagged quietly to the ground. Bill knelt, shook him. It was no use. The guy was asleep. Somewhere in the distance a police siren wailed like a cat on a back fence. It was coming closer. He crouched beside the sleeping man and tried to figure. In another minute it would be too late. It—

Behind him a voice snapped, "What's going on here?"

He turned. Up above him, silhouetted against the light from the street, was a tall man with shoulders built like a mesa. Above the shoulders was a blurred face topped by a wide Stetson.

"Talk up," the big man said.

As the guy spoke he moved a little, and light glinted on a cartridge belt and pistol, on a hunk of star-shaped metal on his left shirt pocket, and on floppy yellow hair spilling out from under the Stetson. Nobody looked that big and important but Deputy Sheriff Carson Smith. When he first met Smith he had taken a dislike to him for no special reason. Now he had a reason. The police sirens sounded very close and Smith was going to cost him his last chance for an alibi.

Or was he? Maybe this was a good time to mix business and pleasure.

He came up from his crouch throwing a long right hook. He wanted to aim it at Smith's jaw but he couldn't afford any luxuries and he opened his hand at the last split-second and smacked the guy across the face with his palm. It was like slapping a hitching post. Then his own head jerked suddenly, jerked again. For a few seconds he couldn't understand what was happening. His head jerked three more times. Finally he got it. The big square shoulders in front of him were twitching as Smith let him have short hard hooks. They hurt. They hurt worse than any punches Russ had thrown. There was a ripping twist on the end of each one.

If this went on much longer he could stop looking for an alibi and start looking for a face. He ducked, charged blindly into the grinding blows, went lurching past Smith and out onto the pavement and tripped and went down in the gutter. Brakes squealed near his head. He lay there panting and saw feet beginning to gather around him. Somebody reached down, hoisted him to his feet, clamped him tight so he couldn't fall.

"What goes on, Carse?" somebody asked.

He got his eyes into focus and saw that he was jammed up against a big easily breathing chest that sported a starshaped hunk of metal. From inside the chest came a rumble and over his head a voice said, "Had to cool down a feller thought it was his night to howl."

"Looks like the guy we had a call on. We'll take him off your hands, Carse."

The chest vibrated again. "Can if you want. Man's a tourist, though. Happened to meet him today and know where he's staying. I could just as easy park him back at the tourist court."

A hand lifted Bill's chin and he saw a cop peering at him. The cop shook his head. "Carse," he said, "you sure do work a man over fast. Well, we have no real charge against him and if he's a tourist and you want to go to the trouble—"

"I don't mind if I do."

"All right, Carse. Mighty obliged."

The cop moved away and the prowl car went into gear and eased off down the street.

"How you feeling, Wayne?" Smith said.

"I'll feel better when you let me breathe."

Smith released him and stepped back a pace and brushed off his shirt. There were some dark splotches on it and Smith looked at them sadly. "Pardner," he said, "you messed up this here shirt."

"Sorry. When I get cut up I have a bad habit of bleeding."

"That's just a bloody nose, Wayne. Ain't hardly worth a mention."

"If you had it I bet it would be worth a mention."

"Seems like I ain't met many fellers can give me one. Got my car down the street, Wayne. Give you a lift back to the court. But first let's take a look at this guy you was scrapping with." He took a firm hold of Bill's arm and led him into the alley and bent to examine the soldier. "Reckon he's all right," he said.

"The MPs will scoop him up. Pardner, seems to me you pick on kinda little fellers."

"I picked on you too, remember?"

"Mighty foolish thing, Wayne. You try that on some peace officers and you could wind up shot. But I don't reckon in the dark you could see who you was jumping. Well, let's mosey to the car."

He led the way down the street. After they climbed into the convertible Smith got a canteen from the glove compartment and splashed water on a handkerchief and handed it over. Bill dabbed at his face with it as the convertible headed back to the tourist court. The wet cloth and cold night wind cut into bruised places like salt. They whisked past the park where the .45 was hidden and raced up to the tourist court and came to a screeching stop at the curb. Smith got out and escorted him toward his room. They had almost reached it when the door of another cottage opened and light washed over them and Holly Clark peered out.

"Evening, ma'am," Smith said, tugging at his Stetson.

"Why, it's Carson!" she cried, as if she had just discovered something very wonderful. "And...and is that Bill Wayne?" First somebody brought a lovely apple to teacher and then she found a worm in it.

"Yes," he said. "Sorry."

She peered at them more closely and gave a little scream. "You're hurt!" she cried. "Oh, look at you!"

"It's not bad," Bill said. "I'm all right."

"You?" she said. "I'm talking about Carson. There's blood all over his shirt! Oh, and look at his poor scraped knuckles! Whatever happened to you?"

"A guy named Wayne," Bill said, "bled on him."

"I don't think that was a very nice thing to do," she said. "Don't tell me you skinned his knuckles too."

"Yeah. With my face."

"What was your face doing there?" she said. "Please come inside and let me fix you up, Carson."

"Shucks, ma'am, it ain't nothing," Smith said, letting himself be towed into her cottage.

Bill followed them inside. He didn't want them getting talkative and swapping a lot of information about him. Holly went to work on Smith as if he had come apart and had to be patted softly together again.

"You're sure your chest isn't hurt?" she asked anxiously.

"His chest is all right," Bill said. "That swelling you see is just manly pride."

"Oh hush!" she said. "Now Carson, the way to get the blood out of your shirt is with cold water. If I gave it a quick soaking right now—"

"I reckon maybe you better not, ma'am," Smith said, his face coloring like a western sunset. "It's like this, well, uh—"

"He doesn't wear an undershirt," Bill said.

She said angrily, "Lots of fine people don't wear undershirts."

In another minute she would have the guy's shirt off

and be swooning over his muscles. Bill didn't think he could stand watching that. "I know," he said, "but Smith might catch cold wearing a damp shirt around at night."

Holly sighed. "I suppose you're right. How do you feel, Carson?"

"Mighty fine, ma'am."

"But if he needs a blood transfusion," Bill said, "call on me. No use wasting all this I'm losing."

"It's nothing but a nosebleed," Holly said. "It's the altitude, six thousand and seventy-five feet. That will do it."

"It was not done by the altitude," Bill said. "It was done by a fist."

"Well, really!" she cried. "If you *will* go downtown and do a lot of drinking—and don't think I can't smell it!—and then get in a fight I don't know what else you can expect. And you don't seem the least bit grateful to Carson for rescuing you."

"He rescued me by deciding not to hit me any more."

Smith said reproachfully, "That don't make it sound very neighborly, Wayne. It was like this, ma'am. Wayne here was beating up a soldier in an alley when I come along."

"A soldier," she said. "Shame on you."

"A small soldier, too," Smith said. "He was the kind of little feller you would think would run twenty to the squad instead of just a dozen. So when I saw this little feller go down, I stepped in to haul Wayne off him. It was dark and maybe I looked small too and Wayne come up from a crouch and hit me. I'll admit I cuffed him around a little. Then the Cheyenne police come by and I talked them out of jailing Wayne, and I brung him back so he wouldn't get in no more trouble."

"I think it was wonderful of you," she said warmly.

"Just bein' neighborly, ma'am," Smith said, getting up. "Well, I got to hit the trail. Might drop by tomorrow mornin' to say goodbye before you folks move on, if you wouldn't mind."

"I wouldn't want to miss saying goodbye," Bill said. "My cottage is the second down the line. If I'm not up when you come around, rap three times on my face and I'll know it's you."

"Please ignore him," Holly said. "I'll be glad to see you, Carson. Our bus won't leave before eight-thirty."

Smith ambled back to his car and Bill went to his own cottage and shut the door. He was studying his face in a mirror, and deciding that worse-looking things had come out of train wrecks, when somebody knocked on the door. He opened it and saw Holly, carrying her first-aid kit.

"Now," she said briskly, "let's get you fixed up."

"Don't bother," he growled. "I can still feel a pulse beating faintly."

"You're not as badly off as you think. Now this bruise—" she touched one on his face and made him wince "—takes away that gaunt look from your cheek."

"I'll ask Smith to slug me on the other side so I balance."

"I didn't hear you deny that you hit him first. Now, we'll prop this door open with a chair so nobody will think anything's wrong, and go to work on you."

He watched her spread out the first-aid kit and start work on his face. "Was that play you were making for Smith on the level?" he asked. "You're too smart a girl to use such a corny line."

"It was all an act," she said. "I'm really madly in love with a gorgeous hunk of stuff named Bill Wayne and I'm trying to make him jealous and—"

"Oh, stop it. You—" Just then she poked one of his bruises. "Stop it!" he said.

"I heard you the first time. Please hold still. And—oh, look at this!"

"What's the matter now?"

"Nothing that can't be fixed with needle and thread."

"Wait a minute. I don't have any cuts that need stitches."

"I'm not talking about your face. I'm talking about the buttons on your jacket. They've been cut off."

Trust her to spot whatever he didn't want noticed.

"You ought to take better care of your clothes. What happened to the buttons?"

"They were all loose when I started out tonight. So I cut them off. I carry needles and thread. I'm quite capable of sewing them on. I'd just as soon doctor myself, too, so if you'll—"

"I'm getting around to you," she said coldly, and began to pat his face with something that felt like the blast of a blowtorch. He squirmed, and she said, "I don't know why you wriggle so."

"It isn't my face going up in flames that I mind. It's just the smell of it charring."

"This is a perfectly harmless antiseptic. I only hope that poor soldier you beat up is getting as good attention. Shame on you, picking on a soldier. I suppose during the war you were one of those officers who had nice safe jobs in the rear and bullied enlisted men whenever you had a chance."

He said angrily, "A safe job in the rear, huh? Listen, I had that lovely safe job of flying the Hump into China and—" He stopped abruptly. Why did he have to tell her that? The papers might mention Russ Nordhoff's war record. And if Holly read the story and remembered what he had just said, the coincidence of Russ having flown the Hump might make her curious. On top of the fact that she knew he had a gun, it might spell murder to her. He stared at the heart-shaped face so close to his. She had gray eyes with sort of gold sparks in them. Her eyes also contained something else: a very alert look. She would remember, all right.

The touch of her fingers became suspiciously gentle and she cooed, "Yes? Go on about the Hump."

"You made that crack on purpose, didn't you? Just to see if I'd blurt out what I did in the war."

The patting turned businesslike again. "You insist on treating me like a stranger who has no right to know what you've been doing. You never tell me anything about yourself when I ask directly. I have to find out some way, don't I? There. I think that fixes you up. By morning you won't look any worse than usual." She stood up.

She walked out with a lilt in her step and with the silly tuft of bright hair at the back of her head wagging impudently. Definitely a dame to worry about.

He closed the door and switched out the light and waited in the darkness for everybody in the tourist court to go to bed. He should have used the time for thinking about his many problems but his head was acting like a bell and thoughts merely clanged around inside it like clappers. At twelve-thirty every cottage was dark. He sneaked outside and worked his way through shadows to U.S. 30 and walked down it to the little park and recovered his .45 and brought it back. After the other four guys learned what had happened to Russ, he might need it badly and very fast. He repacked it in his suitcase. That wasn't really dangerous; if the cops worked up to searching his luggage, a gun more or less wouldn't matter much.

He started to take off the sports jacket and his fingers touched the stubs of threads where the buttons had been. He paused, forced his head to stop chiming and to think. Holly knew the buttons were missing. Suppose he never wore the jacket again. And suppose

Holly read in a newspaper about a Cheyenne murder case in which an important clue was a coat button. Would she make a mountain out of that molehill? Maybe, maybe not. The safe thing to assume, however, was that she would make a whole range of Himalayas— Hump, for short—out of it.

After making sure his window curtains were tightly closed he switched on the light and got out needle and thread. He had a brown coat with buttons nearly the right size and shade. Holly had never seen the sports jacket before tonight, and fortunately it didn't have any sleeve buttons. If he switched buttons from the brown suit she would have no reason to question his statement that the buttons on his jacket had been loose and he had cut them off. Quite a girl, Holly. It was remarkable how she had noticed that they had been cut off, not ripped off. It—

A chill the size of a Wyoming blizzard hit him. Now wait. That middle button must have been ripped off. He picked up the jacket with frostbitten fingers and studied it. The threads of the lowest button had been cut cleanly and of course he had done it. The threads of the top button had been cut cleanly and he had done it. But the threads of the middle button had been…had been…

All right, Wayne, face it. They were cut too. Clean and sharp and straight across. You don't lose a button that way in a brawl. Ragged ends are left. Maybe a bit of fabric is torn. And yet he was ready to swear he had the button when he entered the auto repair shop and didn't have it when he left. What was the answer?

He pictured himself once more diving for the .45, hitting the floor groggily, grabbing the gun left-handed, clawing at the safety catch, blacking out. Five seconds before making the dive his right arm had been so numb he couldn't use it. Did the fingers at the end of that right arm suddenly get clever enough to flick off a safety catch? As he blacked out did he really have beginner's luck shooting left-handed? Did the bullet really lift Russ up and back and drop him eight feet away? All that could have happened. Anything was possible.

It was also possible that somebody who didn't like Russ very much had spied on them. And maybe just as the fight ended the guy walked in with a gun and put it on Russ and leaned down and got the .45 and then coolly shot Russ with it. What sweeter alibi could a man want? Then, just in case the guy Russ had beaten up recovered before the police arrived, the killer reached down and cut off a button of the sports jacket to leave as evidence. Anything was possible. It was a flimsy case, though. He wouldn't want to try to prove it in court. You could say it hung by a thread.

He began cutting off the coat buttons and sewing them on the sports jacket. It took a long time because his fingers kept shaking. It would relieve his mind some to think that he hadn't killed Russ. But he didn't get a very good bargain when he traded in his sense of guilt; in its place, he bought himself a chance to worry about who did the killing. Russ had enemies, all right. Any guy who owns a share of a hot half-million bucks has enemies. Maybe Russ had some others around Cheyenne. But, for the time being, it was enough to list the half-million-dollar ones: Ken in Salt Lake City and Frankie in Reno and Cappy in Frisco and Domenic in L.A.

Russ had been willing to see the other four get knocked off. Maybe one of the others felt the same way and was doing more about it than just hoping. It might be worthwhile to remember his hunch that, ever since leaving Philadelphia, somebody had been tailing him.

Six

The next morning he was up early, shaved what he was using for a face these days, and walked to a roadside diner. The bus was taking some of the other tourists downtown for breakfast but he didn't want to join them and have a post mortem held on his appearance right in the middle of Cheyenne. He climbed onto a stool at the counter and ordered bacon and eggs. The man on his right was reading a newspaper. There might be a story in it about the murder, and Bill leaned closer to take a look. But the newspaper was folded so that only part of two columns of the front page were showing.

The man peered at him warily: an average American greeting the new day as if it had come to the door to collect a bill.

Next to him the average American suddenly snapped the paper all the way open. Eight columns of black headline exploded into sight:

MYSTERY KILLER SHOOTS GARAGEMAN.

Then the guy refolded his paper and got up slowly. Bill trembled.

The average American looked at him sharply, as if he had been reading a few thoughts along with the news. "Here," he said. "You want it? Death and taxes, death and taxes, that's all you get in the paper these days. And the Giants dropped a double-header." He shoved the paper into Bill's sweating hand and walked out.

This called for a little privacy. Bill moved his stuff to an empty booth. His nerves were in pretty good shape; as he made the switch not more than half the coffee spilled into the saucer. He read the story. Shot through the heart…evidence of terrific fight…robbery apparently not motive…body discovered shortly before midnight by so-and-so returning to his home a block away and noting lights still on…somebody heard shot about 9:45 P.M. but it being Cheyenne on Saturday night thought it was just a shot…Sheriff's office investigating and—

Sheriff's office. Apparently Russ's garage was outside city limits. That meant Deputy Sheriff Carson Smith might be working on the case. Coaxing Smith to beat him up had been a good investment; he had a gilt-edged alibi.

He finished breakfast and went back to the tourist court, leaving the newspaper in the diner. The fewer copies that came within range of Holly Clark, the better. As he packed his things he decided to wear the sports jacket, so that Holly would have no reason to think about the buttons that had been missing last night. Then he went outside to wait for the bus to return from the breakfast trip downtown.

He was standing by the bus when a voice drawled, "Howdy there, Wayne. Yuh look right good today. Feel ready to lick yore weight in small boys again?"

Bill looked around. There was Deputy Sheriff Carson Smith, on leave of absence from a dude ranch advertisement. "Hello," he said. "Did your knuckles recover from that severe bandaging they got here last night?"

Smith blew on his knuckles and polished them on his two-toned shirt and admired the luster. "Why shucks, I didn't begrudge the little lady a chance to fix me up. She around?"

"You must be death on rustlers if you chase them the way you chase dames. Don't you ever have any work to do?"

"Well now, we got a little killin' to clean up today, but I don't reckon it'll take too long. I got time to wait." He took a coin from his pocket and flipped it idly and caught it. "Why don't you hop on the bus?" he said. "I don't need yore help in talking to the little lady."

"I'll toss you for it. Heads I stay out of your way. Tails you gallop off in your convertible. Flip your coin and we'll see."

"This?" Smith said. "This ain't no coin, pardner. Look." He thrust out his hand.

Bill stared at the object. It was as nice a thing to have within range of his sports jacket as a grenade with the pin out. It was the missing button. When you looked at it next to the sports jacket you saw that it matched the fabric much better than the set he had sewed on last night. That wasn't the sort of thing the average man was likely to notice. A girl would, though. Especially Holly.

He wet his lips, which felt as if he had been staggering across the plains looking for a waterhole, and said, "What's it supposed to be, a lucky piece?"

"No-o. I reckon you could call it an unlucky piece. Feller done the killin' last night left it behind. That's unlucky for him."

There was a queer glint in Smith's eyes, and for a moment Bill thought it meant something. Maybe the guy was hiding some brains behind that wide-open-spaces look on his face. That would be bad. It might mean that Smith was suspicious of him and was setting a trap. If he fell into any trap Smith set, he was cooked. He wouldn't be able to look for any breaks, such as talking the guy into checking whether Ken or Frankie or Cappy or Domenic had done the killing.

He said carefully, "I should think you'd be out looking for your murderer, instead of standing around here."

"I am looking. Can't hardly tell where he might be. One place is as good as another. It—why, hello there, ma'am." He swung around and smiled at Holly.

"Hello, Carson," she said softly.

Smith gave the button a final flip and put it in his pocket. Bill started catching up on some of the breaths he had skipped in the last minute. That glint in Smith's eyes hadn't meant anything. Obviously all the guy had on his mind was Holly; the way he stared at the girl you might think he had just struck gold. Smith couldn't seem to find any words to express the wonder of it all.

Under any other circumstances Bill might have walked off and let them coo at each other, but he couldn't take the chance that they might trade notes about guns and killings. He said, "Would you like me to make conversation? Reckon it's a nice day, ma'am. It certainly is, Carson. Yore looking' mighty pert this mornin', ma'am. You look glorious yourself, Carson. Why, thank you, ma'am, that makes pore little ugly me feel right good. I—"

"If you start gasping for breath," Holly said between clenched teeth, "I'll be glad to give you a whiff of carbon monoxide."

"Don't mind him, ma'am," Smith said. "Never yet knowed a coyote didn't love to howl. You are lookin mighty pert, though."

"Thank you, Carson," she murmured. "You look glor—I could wring your neck, Bill Wayne!"

Bill said, "I have more conversation you can borrow, when you run through that. Now let's see, Smith still has to use the line about pore little ugly him."

"Let's pretend Mr. Wayne just crawled back under a stone," Holly said. "How are those skinned knuckles of yours today, Carson?"

"You done a fine job on them, ma'am. Look."

Holly took his hand and cooed over the knuckles as if they had just been born. "But you look tired," she said. "It must have worn you out last night handling that drunken Bill Wayne."

"No ma'am. Didn't hardly work up a sweat with him. Thing was, we had a little killin' last night and I been up workin' on it."

"How exciting! Is it all taken care of now?"

"All but catching the feller done the killin', ma'am."

"Oh dear, I wish I had time to hear all about it. I—"

A voice out on the highway called, "Hey, Carse! Where you been?"

An old black coupe had stopped on the road. A man with a face as long and sad as a burro's was leaning out. Smith called back, "Howdy, Sheriff." Then he told Holly, "That there's the sheriff. Wonder what he wants."

Bill said, "Maybe he wants to clean up that little detail of catching the murderer."

"Say now, maybe he does. You want me, Sheriff?"

The sheriff said wearily, "You comin' to do some work? Won't look good if I have to run in one of my own deppities for vagrancy."

"Be right with yuh, Sheriff. Well now, ma'am—"

"I'll never hear about your murder case," Holly said sadly.

"We can fix that, ma'am," Smith said. He walked to his car and brought out the morning newspaper and handed it to her. "Whole yarn's in there," he said.

"That is, except my name. Can't figger how they over-looked that."

"They probably mislaid it," Bill said, "among the comic strips."

"Now and then," Smith said, "I figger I was a mite too gentle with you last night, Wayne. Mebbe we'll be ridin the same trail again some day and I can take care of that. Well, ma'am—"

"Good luck, Carson," she said warmly. "Maybe some day—"

"Shore hope so, ma'am, G'bye." He climbed into the convertible and drove off behind the sheriff's old black coupe.

"And as we ride away into the purple dusk," Bill said, "we say goodbye to that knight of the plains, Deputy Sheriff Smith. But we will always remember him as he stood before us, quick on the trigger and slow in the head."

"I wish," Holly said, "somebody would serve you up barbecued."

She turned away and began getting the party organized to leave. Bill got in the bus and took his usual seat at the back. He kept watching the girl in the hope that she would put down her newspaper and forget about it. She didn't, though. It was still tightly clamped under her arm as the bus started. Holly counted to make sure everybody was aboard, then sat in front and opened the paper.

He got up there fast and slid in beside her. "I hope

you're not really angry," he said. "It was just that I hated seeing a girl with brains and good looks wasting time on Smith."

"I'm not interested in your motives. He was very charming and every time we were getting along nicely you broke it up."

"You know what? I bet he learned how to make time with dames by watching double-feature westerns. That simple-minded cowboy act of his didn't seem quite real."

"I do not care to discuss the subject. I would like to read my newspaper."

"Newspaper!" he said scornfully. "When there's all this gorgeous scenery to watch? Look at those blue hills up ahead."

"I'm looking. What about them?"

"Why, they're beautiful. Like…like distant islands floating on the sea."

"I never saw a dusty sea before."

"Poetic license. And look at those rock shapes to the north. That one's like a crouching panther, and that one is a giant's red castle, and that mesa with the red and blue blotches is…is…"

"It reminds me a little," she said, "of your face last night. When did you get so interested in scenery?"

"Well, you told me I ought to pay some attention to the scenery and so I gave it the old college try and what do you know, it got to me. It's like discovering a new world and wanting to talk about it. You don't mind my talking about it, do you?"

She folded the newspaper and put it down on the far side of the seat. She looked at him the way a cat might study a mouse hole and said, "It seems a bit sudden to me, but however. Well, between Cheyenne and Salt Lake City, which we'll reach tonight, there are about four hundred and sixty-five miles of scenery. If you want me to see it through your newly opened eyes, go ahead."

For the next two hours he gave her a travelogue talk. No pioneer ever had harder going through the cobbled foothills and buttes and mesas. The bus didn't seem to get anywhere; it sat on the road and scrabbled with its tires like a beetle trying to climb up a tilted sheet of glass. A big mountain would park itself far to the north or south and sit there for ages making him spout poetry about it. Every time his ideas started failing, the girl stirred restlessly and reached for her newspaper. He was rewarded finally, though. The bus made a coffee stop in Laramie Valley and Holly joined the others at a lunch counter. The bus driver checked the engine and got his hands greasy, and Bill gave him the outside pages of Holly's newspaper so he could wipe them off.

Seven

At nine o'clock on Tuesday night he bought a ticket and entered a movie theater in Salt Lake City and at a quarter after nine he slipped quietly out through a side exit. He had seen the film in Philadelphia and if anybody asked him he could describe it perfectly. That fact, and the ticket stub which he had saved, ought to give him a good alibi for the next two hours while he paid a call on his old friend and co-pilot, Ken Hayes. Not that he expected the police to come around asking questions. Worse than that. The questions would be asked by Holly Clark.

For the last forty-eight hours he had been trying to get away unobserved and drop in on Ken. If he had kept a diary it would go like this:

Sunday night: Reached Salt Lake City about eight-thirty after driving through canyons that looked as if nothing could move around safely in them except echoes. Unloaded at new tourist court downtown on Main Street. Looked up Ken Hayes in phone book and found he runs a tourist court on outskirts of town off U.S. 40. What a mess if we'd been booked to stay there! Decided to hike couple miles to his place and look situation over. Holly Clark invited herself to go along on walk. Walked long distance trying to exhaust her. Exhausted self.

Monday morning: Counting today we have two days here. Ought to be plenty of time for Ken. At breakfast read Salt Lake *Tribune,* found small story datelined Cheyenne saying sheriff expecting arrest momentarily in garage murder. Holly Clark rounded up everybody for visit to Beehive House, where Brigham Young lived, and Lion House, where some of his wives lived. Places full of history. Also full of Holly Clark. No chance to get away.

Monday afternoon: Tour of Temple Square. Big crowd made it easy to slip away. Made it easy for Holly to slip away too. Caught me in ten steps and I had to pretend great interest in Sea Gull Monument, which marks time when sea gulls rescued crops of pioneers from plague of locusts. Speaking of plagues, hello, Miss Clark. Decided in desperation maybe all she wants is to be fed, like locusts. Invited her to dinner on Starlight Roof of Hotel Utah. Starlight Roof said to be dressy place; Holly dashed off at five to start dressing for dinner at seven. Gave me time to grab taxi, drive out past Ken's tourist court. He's in town, all right. Even caught glimpse of him painting cottages. Sign up: Closed for Redecoration. Very convenient; no one will be around to interrupt. Planning to drop in on Ken late tonight after feeding locusts at Hotel Utah.

Monday night: Holly looked excited as girl going to first prom. Good view of mountains from Starlight

Roof. Good view of Holly in off-shoulder gown. Didn't
realize they had dancing. Naturally Holly wanted to
dance. Tried to wear her out, dancing. Wore out self.

Tuesday morning and afternoon: Tour of city in bus,
and drive to Black Rock to swim in Great Salt Lake.
Couldn't very well dodge this, and anyway daytime not
right for call on Ken. Holly very cute in bathing suit.
Forgot my scars and went in swimming just wearing
trunks. Holly very sympathetic and wanting to know
how I got scars in back and chest. Told her a .45 bullet
during war. She raised eyebrows and said she didn't
know Japs used .45s. Told her it was probably a captured .45. Holly also asked about newly healed scrape
on left side. Is there anything she won't ask about?
Told her I got it in minor auto accident in spring.
Could see her getting ready to ask exactly how a minor
auto accident could have produced such a scrape.
Dove under water to escape her. Got water, 27 percent
salt, in eyes. It stung.

Tuesday night: Last night in Salt Lake City.
Couldn't afford to fool around. Attached self to others
in party for stroll downtown. Holly joined party too.
Mrs. Anders and Mrs. Cooper grabbed Holly to point
out hats in window. Got chance to sneak into movie
without being seen...

He came out of the alley beside the theater and
peered up and down the street. Nobody from the
Treasure Trip party was in sight. Nobody else seemed
to be showing a suspicious interest in him, either.

That was good, if he could bank on it. During the past forty-eight hours he had watched to see if anybody was tailing him. He hadn't been able to spot anyone, even though a few times he had a feeling that a figure had just dodged out of sight. Maybe that was his imagination.

Maybe his imagination had also been kidding him in New York and Chicago. Maybe no one had crept after him to the garage in Cheyenne. It was hard to shrug off some of the unexplained things that had happened in Cheyenne, however, like the middle button that had been cut off his jacket. He wished he could call Frankie in Reno and Cappy in Frisco and Domenic in L.A., without leaving a trail that the cops might some day trace through telephone company records. He was very curious to know if they were all home.

He had to return to the tourist court to pick up his .45 before calling on Ken. Fortunately everybody in the Treasure Trip party was out sightseeing, so he could slip in and get the gun without being spotted. There was a back entrance to the tourist court, and he took it to avoid passing the lighted office at the front. A few of the cottages were lighted, too, but nobody was outside them. His own cottage was in a group of dark ones. He walked quickly toward it. A dim light seemed to be moving in his bedroom but of course that was just a reflection of outside lights on the window glass. It—

He stopped suddenly. The light kept on moving. His heart began punching him in the ribs and his skin started feeling a couple sizes too small for his body. Someone was in his place. He covered the ten steps to the cottage as if walking a tightrope. The flicker went on, soft, misty. It might be a flashlight beam sifting through a handkerchief. The door was open two inches. He eased it open a little more and slid into the room.

At that second the flashlight blacked out.

He couldn't see anything. He couldn't hear anything but the pile-driving thud of his heart. But somebody was almost close enough to touch. It couldn't be a cop. Cops wouldn't have to sneak into his place to search for evidence. It had to be one of his pals. He began crouching. If a bullet came at him it would probably come at belt level. He had to get below that. He crouched lower and lower and heard a board squeak under his shifting weight and then the flashlight beam hit him like the strike of a rattler.

He drove in low and hard. A body slid off his shoulder and went down and he turned and pounced like a cat at the sounds it made hitting the floor. There was a throat somewhere in the blackness. He clamped a hand on it and reached out to grab the head and bash it on the floor. The head didn't feel right. Its hair was soft, sleek, *too long*.

He eased the throat grip. "Who is it?" he gasped.

The throat quivered under his hand. It made a faint

squeaking noise. He got up slowly, all his joints feeling old, and fumbled to the light switch and turned it on. For a few seconds the throat in his grip had been Domenic's or Frankie's or Ken's or Cappy's, and all his troubles had been solved. But the touch of sleek hair, the faint hurt squawk from the throat, had told a different story. His troubles weren't solved. They were getting worse. Slumped on the floor, holding her throat in both hands, was Holly.

He knelt beside her and said anxiously, "Are you hurt? Shall I call a doctor?"

She tried to speak and then shook her head.

"What about this leg? The one that's under you?"

She looked down and saw that her skirt was above her knees and quickly pulled it lower.

"Stop being so damn modest and find out if it's broken!"

She straightened her leg carefully, managed to whisper, "I'm all right. That is…" Her glance flicked toward the foot of his bed, moved back to study his face. "I'm all right," she said, but she didn't sound very sure about it.

He looked at his bed. His suitcase lay on it, open. His clothes had been removed and piled neatly on the bed. Nothing was left in the suitcase but one object. The automatic. He went to the door and closed it and turned to stare at the girl. He didn't really want to question her. He might not like the answers. But the answers would still be in her mind whether he asked questions or not, so he might as well find out how bad they sounded.

"Let's not pretend you were looking to see if any of my socks needed mending," he said. "What's the deal?"

"Bill," she said faintly, "you're scaring me."

"It's time you got scared. You almost had your head cracked open a few minutes ago. Of course it must have had a few cracks in it anyway, to account for this stunt you pulled. Let's see, now. We were downtown with some of the crowd, and as soon as my back was turned, you sneaked away to come here."

"As soon as *your* back was turned? You mean, you sneaked away as soon as *my* back was turned. When I found you had vanished, I figured the only place you could have gone was into that theater. So I described you to the cashier and she said yes, a man like you had just bought a ticket and gone inside."

"So you thought you had a couple hours in which to search my room."

"All right, I admit it. But it turns out that you wanted a couple of hours to do something mysterious, with a movie as your alibi. You went into the theater and only stayed a few minutes and then sneaked out. Why did you come back here, Bill?"

"We're getting a little turned around," he said angrily. "Why did *you* come back here? What were you looking for?"

"That…that gun."

"You already knew about it. You saw it in Cheyenne, the last time you busted into my room without an invitation. I told you I got in the habit of keeping it around during the war. Why did you want to look at it tonight?"

"I wanted to find out," she said in a quavering voice, "if it was forty-five caliber."

He'd expected answers that sounded bad, and he certainly wasn't being disappointed. But maybe if he talked fast enough he could get out of this jam. "All right, so you found it was a thirty-eight. But I don't know why the caliber interested you. I just happen to like a thirty-eight because it has a lighter recoil. It—"

"Bill, that's not true. It says right on the barrel that it's a forty-five."

"If I happened to be a guy you should be scared of, that might be a stupid remark."

"I know. And I'm going to say something that might be even more stupid. Bill, did you kill that man?"

He sat down on the bed to give his legs a chance to stop shaking. He didn't have much hope now of talking his way out of this, but he might as well give it a try. "What man?"

"The man in Cheyenne. Russ somebody."

"I don't know anybody in Cheyenne except that deputy sheriff of yours."

"Bill, there's no use covering up. I read that newspaper. The one telling about the man who was shot and killed by a bullet from a forty-five. Did you think I couldn't see that you were trying to keep me from reading that story? You were awfully obvious, working so hard at entertaining me and finding ways to grab every paper I got my hand on. But you missed one of the papers on the bus. I hid it, and read the story after we arrived here."

"So that's why you've been keeping such a close watch on me lately. You ought to pay your imagination time and a half for overtime."

"It's not imagination! Remember in Cheyenne how you let slip the fact that during the war you flew the Hump? The story about the man who was killed said he flew the Hump too. You wanted the newspapers so that I wouldn't read the story and put those two facts together."

"Thousands of guys flew the Hump. One of them gets bumped off and it's my fault, is it?"

"You have a forty-five caliber pistol. The paper said he was killed by a forty-five caliber bullet."

"Thousands of guys have forty-fives."

"How many of them lost a coat button last Saturday night in the dead man's garage?"

This was worse than he had expected. He sat there, sweating, and remembered how Russ had squirmed under his own questioning that night in the garage. He began to understand how Russ must have felt.

"I told you," he muttered, "that one of the buttons on my coat was loose and I cut it off and—"

"You changed the whole set of buttons on that coat.

The new ones aren't a perfect match. And I saw Carson Smith, the morning we left Cheyenne, with a button in his hand that matched the original ones on your coat. Where did he find it, Bill?"

"The only thing I know about buttons is that you don't seem to have all yours."

"You picked a fight with Carson Smith that night. Why? The paper said there were signs of a big fight in the garage. Were you fighting the man who was killed? Did you get marked up? Did you pick a fight with Carson to have an alibi for the way you looked?"

He said earnestly, "I admit you could get me in trouble with all these wild ideas. But be honest, now. Couldn't the whole thing be in your imagination? Is there a single real fact among any of the things that are bothering you?"

"Bill, *you* be honest. How easy would it be to prove you knew the man who was killed?"

"Suppose I say I never met him in my life. Will you accept that?"

"Bill, I can't! What would happen if somebody called your family and asked casually if you knew him?"

She sat on the floor, hugging her knees and peering at him over the top of them. She looked as if she ought to be out playing hide-and-go-seek instead of grilling a guy about a murder. She looked soft and meek and scared, but she couldn't have thrown nastier questions if she had been a district attorney.

"All right," he muttered. "I knew him."

"I'm only trying to help. I've been sure for quite a while that you're in some awful trouble. But don't you see, I can't go around wondering if...if..."

"Here's the whole story. Or anyway as much of it as I know. Russ was with me in the war. Afterward I started a little commercial airline in China with Russ and a few other guys from my outfit. We started to clear out in '49 when the Reds moved in, but I got shot by some crazy soldier and couldn't make the plane and was left behind. I didn't get home until last spring."

"It was a soldier who shot you, and not one of the men working with you?"

"I said so, didn't I? When I got back home, one of the papers did an interview with me. The day after it was published I got a queer phone call. From a guy whose voice I couldn't recognize. He wanted to know the addresses of the men who'd been with me in China. When I started asking questions, he first offered me a thousand bucks for the addresses, then started making threats. I laughed at him. He said I must be in on the deal with them, and that I'd be sorry. He hung up. That night somebody took a shot at me."

"Did that make the mark on your side? The one you claimed you got in an auto accident?"

"Yeah. So I decided I'd better take a trip and find my pals and see what the trouble was, and warn them somebody was gunning for us. I was on my way to visit Russ that night, and somebody slugged me outside his garage. When I came to, Russ had been killed by a bullet from my gun. Now you see what a mess it is."

He had been reciting the story fast in the hope that its weak points would zip past too quickly for her. The look on her face said that hadn't worked. Probably one of her first-grade pupils could get the same reaction from her by reciting two times two is five, two times three is nine, two times four is six.

"Why," she asked, "didn't you telephone your friends to warn them, instead of making a long trip?"

"For one thing I didn't know their exact addresses."

"Long-distance telephone operators are awfully clever at locating people."

"I was a little worried about what the boys had been up to. I figured if I dropped in on them without warning—"

"Why did you sign up for this tour, instead of going directly by car or train?"

"In case the boys had pulled something really bad, I didn't want to leave a big trail tying myself to them. This tour sort of covered up what I was doing."

"You hadn't been with them since 1949. How could you be blamed for any trouble they got into since then?"

He couldn't take much more of this. She was cutting him up into little wriggling pieces. "I didn't know the score. I didn't want to take any chances."

"One of them lives here in Salt Lake City, doesn't he? You've been trying to slip away ever since we got here."

"Well, yes. I've got to find out what's happening. I—"

"You came back here tonight to get your gun before visiting him, didn't you?"

"This is a nasty business. I'm not going to get caught short again."

"Bill, after you found that man had been killed, why didn't you call the police?"

"When a guy's been shot with my gun? I'd probably have to take the rap for it."

"They'd need more proof than that to convict you of murder. They'd have to prove a motive. Were you afraid they could find one?"

She had backed him into a blind alley. Every time he tried to find a way out, he ran into another of her roadblock questions. "Guys have little arguments. You never know what the cops might make out of them."

"They could make a lot out of what you've told me."

"The important thing right now is, what do you make out of it?"

She said solemnly, "The only completely honest thing you've said is that you're in a mess."

"Look, Holly, I need a break. I need one bad. Are you going to give it to me?"

"But you haven't given me one! You haven't told me the truth!"

He got up suddenly. This was a waste of time. His only chance was to grab Ken and get the story out of him, before Holly worked herself up to calling in the police. "If I told you the truth," he said, "you wouldn't believe it either." He walked out.

Behind him Holly called something but he didn't stop to listen. Maybe it was a threat to call the police. He wouldn't blame her. A smart girl would have yelled for cops long ago. He cut across Main Street and headed east. The ground began tilting up and up, climbing to one of the Benches where in some past age Great Salt Lake had paused in its steady shrinking. He walked fast, his steps keeping time to a chant that kept pounding in his head: he's-got-to-talk-he's-got-to-talk-he's-got-to-talk…

He realized that he had forgotten the .45. But that might be just as well. Ken wasn't big and husky, like Russ had been. If necessary he could take the guy bare-handed, and now he wouldn't have to worry about a gun going off accidentally in a scrap. Besides, he didn't really think Ken had done any of the shooting. Ken had been a good Joe once. A little weak, maybe, but a good Joe. If Ken would talk sense about who did the shooting in China, and who might have done it in Philadelphia and Cheyenne, there needn't be any real trouble. But trouble or no trouble, Ken had to talk, and talk fast. Back in the tourist court on Main Street, Holly might be calling the cops right now.

He reached level ground where the Bench began and walked over to the street off U.S. 40 where Ken's tourist court was located. Everything in the tourist court was dark except the office. Ken was in there; now and then he saw a shadow moving past the drawn shades. It was a good break that Ken had closed the place for redecoration, because it wouldn't have been easy to jump the guy in a crowded tourist court. He crept to the front door and turned the knob gently. The door was locked. He slipped around the building and found a back door and tested it. The latch slid easily out of the keeper and the door opened.

He stepped inside and put his hand on the inside knob to close the door. A string was tied to the inside knob. His fingers touched it and his nerves screamed a warning and the lights flashed on and there was Ken crouched against a wall with a gun aimed at his guts.

Ken was slim and dark, and his eyes looked like blots of ink on his white face. "I been waiting for you," he said tonelessly. "I—" His eyes seemed to focus for the first time. The gun wobbled and he said, as if talking to himself, "It can't be Bill Wayne. It can't be! He's dead. Way back in China. I'm not going to start seeing things."

It was a long jump to that gun. Ken might be seeing ghosts but his gun wasn't. "Take it easy," Bill said softly. "It's Bill, and I'm alive." The guy was wound up like a clock spring. You had to release the tension slowly.

"You were dead," Ken said, but now he sounded doubtful. "You were flat on your face and I tried to lift your shoulder and it was like heaving at the corner of a sack of flour, you know? So I let you flop down again."

"I got over it. A couple of Chinese carted me away. I didn't get back to the States until last spring."

Ken said wearily, "I thought one of the others must be pulling a fast one on me. That's a bad crowd, not like when you were with us. Grabbing for that lousy gold and seeing it squirt away like watermelon seeds every time you think you have a grip on it does something to guys. Now somebody's always pulling a fast one, always coming up with things."

Bill edged closer, as if walking on broken glass with bare feet. He murmured, "What kind of things?"

"We got a lake we're trying to buy up. You don't know about it. But we need it for a very important reason, see? And I got an idea somebody in the crowd has been buying some of the land under a fake name so he can make the rest of us pay through the nose. Then take this thing about Russ Nordhoff."

"What about Russ?"

"I guess you wouldn't know that either. He got knocked off, Bill. Last Saturday night in Cheyenne. That's one less to cut in on the lake deal, see? One of the crowd has been getting impatient, see? Maybe I'm next on the list."

It was hard to tell whether Ken had cracked completely or had merely been shaken up and might come out of it any minute. Ken wasn't putting down that gun, though. The guy kept making quick nervous gestures with it. The bomber pilots used to have to sweat it out like this, coming back from a mission with a bomb that was armed but had failed to drop. Make a rough landing, and blooie! Trying to jump Ken right now might be the roughest kind of landing. He said, "You were all set for whoever came, weren't you? Clever rig you dreamed up."

"Yeah," Ken said eagerly. "Not bad, is it? I lock the front door so nobody can get in there, see? I leave the back door unlocked. But I tie a string to the knob and run it into the front room. Then I sit here with this other string tied to the main one, you know? Like fishing and waiting for a bite." He jerked at the cross string he was holding in his left hand.

"Didn't give you much time to sleep, did it?"

"Sleep? I don't know what it is any more. I haven't closed my eyes since I read about Russ in the paper. I kicked everybody out of my cottages and pretended to paint them so I could lay a trap. Look. You haven't seen the best part yet." He moved like a squirrel flicking around a tree trunk and closed the back door and scurried to the front room. He moved so fast there was no chance to grab him. He beckoned with the gun.

Bill walked to the front room. Several cords criss-crossed it. One stretched to the back door. Another slanted across the room parallel to the windows, and on it hung a piece of stiff cardboard cut to resemble the silhouette of a man's head and body.

"Look," Ken said. "I sit in the back room with my fishing line, see? I tighten it like this, see, and that cardboard slides down the string and crosses the windows in front of the light. Nice shadow effect, huh? Anybody is watching, I'm walking across in front of the windows. I loosen up on my string and the shadow slides back down the line. I'm quite a web spinner, huh? Walk into my tourist court said the spider to the fly. And who should walk in but old Bill Wayne." He let out a thin laugh.

"Quite a letdown," Bill said. "Put that gun away and let's have a good talk, shall we?"

This was one of those dreams where you feel everything has happened before. Come to think of it, this *had* happened before. But the other time he had been the one with the gun and Russ had done the coaxing.

"I don't know about that," Ken said. "If I put away this gun, one of the other guys might sneak in and I wouldn't be ready for him. Let's just sit down like this." He lowered himself into a chair as if afraid he might break, and motioned Bill to sit in a chair on the other side of the table. He sat silently for a few moments, his eyes as dull as charcoal. "Little foggy," he said. "Too much Benzedrine and not enough sleep. Maybe you're wondering what this is all about, huh?" His eyes seemed brighter now.

If Ken's eyes got back to normal his brain might start clicking too. That would be a bad moment. "Yeah," Bill said. "I'm wondering."

"We gave you a raw deal," Ken muttered. "Then we started giving each other a raw deal. I guess that's natural, huh? I'll tell you about it. Only keep an eye on that string leading to the back door. I don't want to get what Russ got. Guess you don't either."

"I sure don't. I already collected enough slugs from forty-fives. I—"

"What did you say, Bill?"

He stared at the guy. Ken's eyes looked hot and bright enough to burn holes in his head. He had just made a bad mistake with Ken. Maybe the last one he'd have a chance to make. He tightened his leg muscles for a spring, said hoarsely, "You told me Russ was shot with a forty-five and so I—"

"No I didn't! I didn't even say he was shot. So you know all about it, huh? Look who walked into my trap. Good old Bill Wayne and his forty-five. Where is your forty-five, Bill? Gonna reach for it?"

"I don't have a gun," he cried. "Take it easy, Ken. I—"

Ken rose slowly. "You should have stayed dead over in China," he said. "That would have saved me trouble." The revolver lifted, steadied.

Just then a freezing noise crept through the room. A whisper of sound, like a snake crawling through wet leaves. Ken began to shake. Across the room, dipping and swaying in a grotesque dance, came the cardboard silhouette on its string. Behind it the shadow oozed across the drawn shades. Somebody had opened the back door.

Bill slammed the table into Ken and sent him crashing into a corner and made a lunge for the revolver. At almost the same second a scream knifed into his ears, a scream pitched so high it hurt. He wrenched the gun from Ken and whirled toward the back room. Standing in the entrance between the two rooms was a figure with hand clamped to mouth to block another scream. A girl. She had bright hair ending in a tuft at the back of her head. This was the maddest thing that had happened yet. It was Holly Clark.

"Come on in," he said harshly. "We're all crazy here and you'll feel right at home. This is Ken Hayes and he has a persecution complex. My trouble is I'm feeble-minded."

Holly didn't say anything. She stood motionless with her hand still pressed to her mouth. From over in the corner Ken gasped, "Go ahead, sister, scream! Yell for the cops. Yell for anybody. This guy's a killer."

Bill said, "She walks in while you're fixing to shoot me so that makes me a killer."

Ken said, "I don't know you, sister. But if you can't scream you better run."

The girl seemed to be wavering, and Bill said quickly, "Don't, Holly. I was sunk when you walked in. Call the cops and I'm sunk again."

"He admits it," Ken said. "You heard him, didn't you? Do you know why he'd be sunk? Because a guy got killed last Saturday night."

Holly's hand came down slowly from her mouth and she said, as if reciting a lesson, "It was in Cheyenne and his name was Russ Nordhoff."

"I won't ask if you know who killed him," Ken said. "Might not be healthy to say right out loud."

"I don't know who killed him," she whispered.

Bill gave his head a hard shake, the way you might jiggle an alarm clock to start it working. Things had moved too fast for him. Maybe anything that moved at all was too fast for him. He thought that he had left the girl back on Main Street, getting ready to call the police. Instead, here she was, trying to defend him.

Ken said, "If you don't know, I'll tell you. This guy right here killed Russ. If he don't have you hypno- tized, get out while you can. He's a murderer."

"It's not murder if it's in self-defense," she cried. "How do I know what happened in Cheyenne? How do you?"

Ken said, "I know because he sneaked in here to kill me too. Only I was waiting for him and got the drop first."

"Where's my gun?" Bill said. "Where's the gun I was going to shoot you with?"

"Maybe you were gonna vary it a little this time," Ken said. "Maybe you were gonna choke me, or bash in my head." He leered at Holly and said, "You ever been strangled yet, sister? Stick around and maybe you'll find out how it feels."

Bill saw a shudder wrench at the girl's body. He broke open the revolver and knocked the bullets into his hand and put the gun in one pocket and the car- tridges in another. "Holly," he said, "I'll give you two choices. Sit down and listen to the whole story, or call the cops. You can do both if you want."

"Is it going to be the truth this time?" she asked.

"Yeah. But I told you before, it won't sound very good."

She came in and sat on the edge of a chair with her knees pressed tightly together and her fingers laced in a knot. You might think she was ten years old and had been sent to the principal's office for whispering in class. "I'll listen," she said.

Ken was still sprawled on the floor in a corner. He sat up now and stuck his legs straight out and patted his hands together mockingly and said, "Now we get a bedtime story. Once upon a time there was a dreat big nice pilot named Bill Wayne who—"

"I'll give you a choice, too," Bill said. "Shut up or I'll kick your teeth in."

"You'll kick them in anyway. But go ahead."

He gave them the story. It was the first time he had tried to put it all together for anybody and he could see that the result was sort of ramshackle. If he had tried to put together a house that way it would never have rated a loan from a bank. More likely the local zoning board would have ordered him to tear down that eyesore. The trouble was, he was a little short of material. As he talked, Holly watched him with big puzzled eyes. Ken sat in his sprawled legs-out position, looking like the villain in a puppet show. Bill finished the story in a rush. "That's it," he said. He knew he was giving the impression of running away from the thing quickly before it could fall down around his ears.

Holly swallowed once or twice, and said, "What it amounts to is, you went to the garage to make Russ talk, and there was a fight and you don't know whether you shot him or not."

"What it amounts to," Ken said, "is what you get when you skin a zero."

Bill muttered, "Maybe you'd better call the cops, Holly."

"Now just one moment!" she said. "It seems to me you give up very easily. Just as a start, nobody denies they shot you that time in China, do they?"

Ken rattled out a laugh. "Meet nobody, sister. I wasn't even there when he was shot. Ask the other five, only of course you can't ask Russ now, and they'll tell you the same thing. We were away and came back to the field and the dope had got himself shot."

"The hell you weren't there," Bill said.

"Yeah? Prove it."

Holly said angrily, "You know he can't prove a thing, but that doesn't mean it isn't true. Who shot at him in Philadelphia?"

"He made that up."

"He made up a new scar on his left side," she said. "I saw it today when we were in swimming."

"Speaking of swimming," Bill said, "where's that lake where you ditched the plane?"

"I never ride in airplanes," Ken said. "It's too dangerous."

"Don't get so tough with me, Ken."

"Why not? You aren't going to shoot me with this dame watching. You won't even beat me up as long as she's around. Why don't you dust out of here? I'm not going to tell you anything. I don't even know my own name."

"When you call the cops they might want to know it."

"I gave up that idea," Ken said. "I gave it up when I saw you'd lost your nerve about shooting me. So now I don't want cops. You don't want cops. If the girl don't want cops either, let's just sneer at each other and call it a night."

"You could be making an awful mistake."

"Yeah? As how?"

"If I did shoot Russ I might sneak back here to shoot you."

"I'll take the chance."

"Then," Bill said softly, "there's the possibility that I didn't shoot Russ. And if I didn't, you may have another visitor. You won't need cops after he leaves. But you may need an undertaker."

"You can't scare me into talking. Go haunt somebody else."

The girl leaned forward and looked earnestly at Ken and said, "You might be able to clear up the whole horrible mess by talking."

"I don't get your angle at all," Ken said. "Not unless

you're shopping for a husband and figure this guy's better than nothing."

She took a deep breath and said, "I think I understand why people might want to shoot you."

"Ah, run along," Ken said. "You're wasting time you could use holding hands with him."

Bill got up. "Let's go, Holly," he said. "Unlock the front door." He dug out the revolver and reloaded it while she opened the door. Then he said, "Don't try following us, Ken. They haven't raised the price of murder yet. I can still knock off two guys for the price of one." He pushed the girl through the doorway and backed out after her, watching Ken. As he closed the door he caught a final glimpse of Ken sitting motionless on the floor, a puppet waiting for somebody to pull the strings.

He walked rapidly along the side street toward U.S. 40, hardly conscious of the girl's efforts to keep up with him.

"Things haven't changed much," she gasped, "since I was that fat little girl with bangs and a Dutch bob. I still seem to be tagging after you. I still can't quite keep up."

"You'd be smart to run on ahead and stay away from me," he said bitterly. "You'd be smarter to call a cop. I'm in a bad jam and you're trying to get in it with me."

"You didn't kill that man in Cheyenne."

"How do you know? I don't even know if I did it or not."

"I know, that's all. And you need help."

"I can't imagine why you bother."

"It started a long time ago," she said, almost angrily. "Just a silly kid idea of wanting you to notice me, of wanting to do something important for you that would make you take notice. I don't seem to have got over it. I get so mad at myself for feeling like that. Take those times I played up to Carson Smith. When I thought about it I realized I just wanted to irritate you into paying attention to me. It—"

He stopped, grabbed her shoulders. "Look here," he said. "You're not going to do anything idiotic like getting serious about me, are you?"

"Please don't worry. It's merely a sort of challenge, like trying to complete a jigsaw puzzle. Once I finish the job I'll be delighted to kick the thing to pieces. I—"

A sound slapped their ears. A flat ugly sound that lashed through the night and picked up tumbling echoes. Her shoulders went rigid under his hands.

"Stay here," he said.

"Bill! It was a car backfiring!"

He didn't waste time arguing. He turned and raced back toward the tourist court. The place was a quarter-mile away and as he came closer he saw other figures running from neighboring houses and converging on it. He ran into the driveway. Several people were already in front of Ken's office. They were looking down. What they looked at was sprawled on the office steps.

It didn't look as if Ken had moved a foot after the bullet hit him. He seemed more than ever like a puppet as he sprawled on his office steps, but this time you could jerk all the strings in the world and he wouldn't move.

Eight

He stared at the dead man and didn't feel very alive himself. The fact that somebody else had shot Ken proved that somebody else killed Russ in Cheyenne. In one way that was a relief. But in another way it put him in a worse spot than ever. The police wouldn't agree that somebody else had done both killings; they had every reason to pin both on him, if they got a chance.

And on top of that it meant that his vague hunch was correct. Frankie or Domenic or Cappy had trailed him from Philadelphia to New York, and to Chicago. One of them knew all about the Treasure Trip tour and the route he was following. One of them had waited in Cheyenne for him to visit Russ, and had waited here for him to visit Ken. The same guy would be waiting for him farther along the route. He was providing Frankie or Domenic or Cappy with a license to murder.

He said to one of the men standing around Ken's body, "What happened?"

"I don't know," the man said. "I live down the street. Earlier tonight I heard a scream and thought it came from here, but I walked by and nothing seemed wrong. Then I heard the shot and I was on edge from the scream earlier so I ran out. Funny how fast people can gather, isn't it? Did somebody call the police?"

"My wife is phoning them," another man said.

There was no use hoping one of the spectators had seen Frankie or Domenic or Cappy. Whoever did the shooting was too smart to make any mistake like running wildly away down the street.

He eased away from the little group and walked back along the street and bumped into Holly. "All right," he said harshly. "Beat it. Fast."

"Was it…was it…"

"It was. He's dead."

She stared up at him. Her face had a pale drowned look and she touched his arm to steady herself. "Dead," she said in a wondering tone. "Dead." Her mind seemed to be circling the idea the way you might tiptoe around a sleeping tiger. "You did say…dead?"

He was in an impatient mood and wanted to get her out of the way. "D for done in, e for extinct, a for assassin, and d for dear departed. Now beat it, will you? I'm going back there."

"But what for? What can you do now? The police might ask you questions and get suspicious. You can't afford that. Don't you understand, this proves it was somebody else who shot that man in Cheyenne. You've got a real chance to clear yourself. But you can't do it if the police grab you."

"Quit arguing, will you? The cops will be here any

moment and I don't want you involved. I'll keep you out of it. I haven't seen you all evening."

For some odd reason she began to look angry instead of stunned and scared. "I like to get things straight," she said. "Do I understand that you're going to wait for the police and give yourself up?"

"That's right."

"You don't think they'll believe your story, do you? Without a single witness to back you up?"

"They wouldn't believe my story *with* a witness, if you're thinking of trying to be one."

"But Bill, you're giving up without a fight."

He said patiently, "I'm not letting you get into this any deeper. There's a guy loose around here who's better at murder than you are at first-grade spelling."

"I don't like murderers. I don't like them when they're in jail and I like them even less when they're loose."

"You don't understand! I'm this guy's license for murder. I'm his alibi. I'm the decoy who lures ducks into his shooting gallery. As long as I'm walking around free, he can knock off anybody remotely involved in the case and I'll get tagged for it. He could shoot you right now and send the bill to me. So I'm going to the police."

"All right," she said grimly, "then so am I. You were with me that whole evening in Cheyenne, except that we had a quarrel downtown and you went off to get drunk and picked a fight with Carson Smith. We've been together every minute this evening. You've had a nervous breakdown and aren't responsible for anything you say."

"You wouldn't dare lie like that!"

"Wouldn't I? Just wait and see if I don't. Now are you going to be sensible?"

He was certainly not going to break his record by starting to be sensible now. He was going to tell off this vixen and…and…wait a moment! Why was he allowing her to take his arm and lead him down the street away from Ken's place? What was he thinking of, to let her get away with this? Why was he allowing that police car to go wailing by without yelling for it to stop and pick up a quick solution to the case? How—

"Oh, stop dragging back on my arm," Holly said. "You act like a lamb being led to the slaughter. Actually you're being dragged away from it."

"I hope," he grumbled, "the man you marry is a good tough superintendent of schools who can keep you in your place. Do you realize you're likely to get tagged as an accessory after the fact, if I get arrested?"

"But Bill, in this case exactly what is the fact?"

"I'm not prepared to answer that question, teacher."

"You're not prepared for anything! Here you've got a problem and it looks hard and you throw up your hands and say you can't do it. I've known first-graders who didn't give up that easily. Now let's put all the figures down on a blackboard and see if we can't make sense out of them. Which one of your crowd could have done the shootings?"

"There are only three left. Frankie Banta in Reno and Cappy Judd in Frisco and Domenic Ferrante in L.A. I can't quite see Frankie as a gunman. That narrows it down to Cappy and Domenic."

"All right. Now which of them was the leader of the crowd?"

"What do you mean, the leader?"

"Let's take the trouble in China," she said. "Which one of your crowd was capable of working out the plan for stealing that gold? Which one was smart enough to talk the others into it and to explain away any doubts and fears they had? Who made all the big decisions? Back in China, who realized you had to be shot, and did it right then? When you got back home safely this spring, who decided to get rid of you right away?"

"I never thought of it like that. I can't quite fit any of them into that pattern."

"But Bill, one of them had to be the leader. You must have known them very well. Pick the leader and you have the murderer."

That was odd. Come to think of it, none of them had been a real leader. They had always waited for him to make the plans and decisions. "I can't pick the right one," he said.

"Well, who was the other man who used to hang around with your crowd?"

"What other man? There were only five besides me. I named them all for you."

"Then why did that man who was just killed talk as if there was one more? I remember very distinctly what he said. He claimed that he wasn't even present that time in China when you were shot. He said to ask the other five and they'd tell you the same thing, except that of course you couldn't ask Russ. The other *five!* Russ, and the man in Reno, and the one in San Francisco and the one in Los Angeles. That's only four. So who else could you ask?"

"Ken must have made a mistake. Slip of the tongue. There isn't anybody else. There—"

He paused. The idea was prowling through his head like a burglar. It was a disturbing idea and he didn't want it around. Perhaps if he didn't give it any trouble the idea would go away.

Holly watched his face, and said, "Wouldn't that be an odd mistake for Ken to make? If only five men were involved in shooting you and stealing that money in China, Ken must have thought thousands of times about the other four. Were the other four playing fair with him? Would any of the other four get drunk and talk too much? The other four this, the other four that. It would be fixed so firmly in his mind that he *couldn't* make a slip, any more than he could forget his own name. But if there were *five* others besides Ken, that number would be fixed just as firmly in his mind. He would find himself talking about five others even when he didn't mean to."

"It's crazy," he muttered. "My five pals were the only ones in that operations shack we had at the airfield. I finished telling them off, and walked out of the office and took a few steps toward the plane and—"

"Couldn't somebody have been outside the office, lounging against the wall and listening to the quarrel? Somebody who had tipped off your bunch about what the black market man had in those boxes? Somebody who wasn't going to let you mess up his plans?"

"I didn't see anybody."

"You were angry. Maybe you weren't keeping your eyes open."

"No," he said, "I can't go for your idea. You're trying to make a lot out of very little. Give you a splinter and you want to build a house."

"There's nothing wrong with that. It's called scientific method. I admit I'm only a grade school teacher but I certainly know how to apply scientific method to a problem. It's no different than finding a fossil tooth and reconstructing a prehistoric man from it."

"You don't have a tooth and you're constructing a superman."

"Not at all. He merely thinks faster than you do. That doesn't make him a superman. Oh. I thought of one more argument. You said you had a feeling somebody was trailing you back in New York and Chicago. If it was one of the five men in your bunch, wouldn't you have spotted him?"

"Yeah, I should have been able to spot any of the

boys. But don't try to sell me your mystery man on that basis. I'm just not as good at spotting people as I thought. Look at the way I let you trail me to Ken's place tonight, and never realized it."

"But you weren't looking for me, Bill. You were so upset you weren't thinking that somebody might be following you."

He said irritably, "You worry about your mystery man. I'll worry about Cappy and Domenic. One of them did the shooting."

"All right," she said with a small sigh. "I was just trying to help."

They walked on silently for a while. When they passed the opening of a storm sewer, Bill took out the revolver and wiped it carefully and dropped it in the opening. He didn't want to be caught with a weapon that had belonged to Ken. Thinking about pistols reminded him of his own .45, and he asked, "Did you close my suitcase and shut the door when you left my room?"

"I think I did, Bill. Anyway I remember throwing your clothes back into the suitcase to hide that gun."

"I'm glad you have that much sense. But did you ever think what might have happened to you tonight? You trailed a guy who might have been a murderer to that closed and deserted tourist court, and you hung around outside in the dark and—"

"I admit I was scared. But you didn't have a gun and I felt sure you weren't a murderer and were in trouble and needed help."

He said in a wondering tone, "How you've managed to live so long…"

They reached their tourist court on Main Street and turned in the entrance. He thought of something, and said, "Did you wipe off my forty-five after you touched it?"

"Well, no. I didn't think of it."

"If you're going to play around with murder, don't leave prints on murder weapons. Let's get them off right now." He opened the door of his cottage and switched on the light.

"I just thought of something," Holly said. "The man in Cheyenne was shot with a bullet from your gun, of course. But the man tonight was shot with a bullet from another gun. So the police can't possibly connect the two cases. And if they ever ask, I can swear your gun was here all evening."

He fumbled through the suitcase. "You can?" he said.

"Why, of course."

"Then you'll be lying," he said, straightening slowly and painfully. "The thing is gone."

Nine

The bus tires sizzled over the blacktop surface of
U.S. 40, rolling west. The sound drilled into his head
and buzzed around as if somebody were holding a
roller derby up there. He stared glumly out of the bus
window. North of the road the white tablecloth of
Bonneville Salt Flats stretched tight across the land,
covering everything but a toothpick line of telephone
poles in the foreground and the blue scallops of mountains in the distance. The country was just about as
blank as his mind.

Three seats ahead of him, Holly had stopped beside
George M. Blakeslee and was saying tonelessly, "These
are the Bonneville Salt Flats. Way out there they have
auto speed trials on a fourteen and one-half mile
straightaway. Sir Thomas Lipton holds the record for—"

"Lipton?" Blakeslee said. "He was the yacht man.
Used to challenge for the America's Cup with yachts
he always named Shamrock. Never heard of him
racing autos."

Holly murmured vaguely, "I don't know why I said
that, Mr. Blakeslee. John Cobb set the record. Three
hundred and ninety-four and two-tenths miles an
hour. He did it in 1947."

Get 2 Books Every Month...
For the Price of ONE!

☐ **YES! Sign me up for the Hard Case Crime Book Club!**

As long as I choose to stay in the club, I will receive TWO Hard Case Crime books each month — that month's latest title plus an earlier title from the Hard Case Crime archives. I'll get to preview each month's titles for 10 days. If I decide to keep them, I will pay only $6.99* each month — a savings of 50%! There is no minimum number of books I must buy and I may cancel my membership at any time.

Name: _____

Address: _____

City / State / ZIP: _____

Telephone: _____

E-Mail: _____

☐ **I want to pay by credit card:** ☐ VISA ☐ MasterCard ☐ Discover

Card #: _____ Exp. date: _____

Signature: _____

Mail this card to:
HARD CASE CRIME BOOK CLUB
20 Academy Street, Norwalk, CT 06850-4032
Or fax it to 610-995-9274.
You can also sign up online at www.dorchesterpub.com.

* Plus $2.00 for shipping. Offer open to residents of the U.S. and Canada only. Canadian residents please call 1-800-481-9191 for pricing information.

If you are under 18, a parent or guardian must sign. Terms, prices, and conditions subject to change. Subscription subject to acceptance. Dorchester Publishing reserves the right to reject any order or cancel any subscription.

"Man must be crazy to drive that fast," Blakeslee said. "That must be almost as fast as a bullet."

Bill stared at the back of the man's head and thought: no, Blakeslee, not nearly as fast as a bullet. With one type of load, a forty-five caliber bullet has a muzzle velocity of 1800 feet per second. That works out to 1200 miles an hour. According to this morning's edition of the Salt Lake *Tribune*, a guy named Ken Hayes found out the hard way last night how fast a .45 bullet moves. If anybody asked me nicely for the serial number of the gun used in the shooting, I think I could provide it. Unfortunately I couldn't provide the gun. Somebody borrowed it last night and forgot to return it.

Holly was saying, "...and so when Great Salt Lake retreated it left these flats. I understand they're twenty-seven percent salt."

"Now wait a minute," Blakeslee said. "They ought to be almost a hundred percent salt. Aren't you thinking of the water in Great Salt Lake?"

"I suppose I am," Holly said. "I don't know where my mind is today." She walked past Blakeslee and came back to Bill and said in a mechanical voice, "Can I do anything for you?"

Maybe he could snap her out of the trance. "Yes," he said in a loud cheerful tone. "Please pass the salt."

Up ahead in the bus, several people caught his remark and got a chuckle out of it. It didn't take much to make people laugh: look at television. Holly turned red and whispered angrily, "How can you make a joke of things?" She walked away with firm steps, as if trampling him underfoot, and began showing her usual brisk skill in running the tour.

That was fine. Now if somebody would kindly crack a whip over this character Bill Wayne and get him to show his usual brisk *lack* of skill, everything would be back to normal. He wished he had an idea what to do. He didn't ask for a brilliant idea. Any old beat-up notion would be welcome. If things went on like this there would be more killings, and somewhere in the future a bullet was waiting for him. He was a valuable asset to the killer only while he blundered ahead on the road to Reno and San Francisco and Los Angeles, providing an alibi for more murder. If he tried to leave the road, however, his usefulness would be over and Cappy or Domenic—whichever it was—would want to get rid of him. At the end of the road his usefulness would also be over, and he would be knocked off quickly so that he could be publicly blamed for all the murders. The road west was like a conveyor belt dragging him toward murder.

Those were unpleasant thoughts. In case they were lonely in his head, he might add to them the thought of what might happen to Holly when No-Gun Wayne died with his two-toned shoes on.

Today's run was taking them from Salt Lake City to a place in Nevada called Winnemucca, about 365 miles. They had started early, to avoid midday heat in the desert, and the day stretched endlessly in back of him and into the future. He tried to forget things by watching the country.

Ahead in the bus, Holly was announcing, "In case any of you wonder about these trails leading into the mountains, a great many of them go to old mines. Or maybe to new ones, too. There really is gold in those hills."

Indeed there is, he thought. Half a million dollars' worth, in one spot. His five pals had been heading for Bonneville Salt Flats when they ran out of gas and ditched in a lake. Probably quite a distance north and to the west, though. There wasn't enough water around here for a duck to make a forced landing. He stared moodily out of the window and watched dust devils doing a ballet. They whirled over the hot dry ground like dust rising behind a phantom posse. Speaking of posses—

He looked back down the miles of blacktop road. Far behind was a truck-trailer flying a plume from the exhaust of its diesel. Nothing to worry about there. But back of the truck was a sedan, coming very fast. An optimist would laugh at the idea that the sedan was filled with Nevada State Police coming to arrest him. He wished he knew an optimist. He watched the sedan overtake them. It contained a man, a woman and two children.

He sighed and started to relax and then spotted another suspicious car. He didn't want to watch it but it was very difficult to turn away and feel it creeping up behind him. And there was one advantage in watching for police cars: it passed the time. He made a game out of it, scoring a point against himself every time he worried about a harmless car. By the time they reached Winnemucca in the late afternoon he was behind by a score of thirty-one to nothing.

The town of Winnemucca was about six gas stations long by four taprooms wide. But the place had quite a hotel. It was sleek and modern and had a tiled patio decked with gay umbrellas around a swimming pool. He relaxed in his air-conditioned bedroom and studied the play of light on the swimming pool below his window and on the Tom Collins glass in his hand. Things were going to look brighter as soon as he got outside the Tom Collins and inside the swimming pool. He changed slowly into a bathing suit and went outside.

The first person he saw was Holly coming out of the water. She wore a two-piece white bathing suit and an air of assurance. That added up to more assurance than bathing suit. She had long slim legs and a flat stomach and hips that at one moment were all angles, like a coat hanger, and at the next were all curves. It was odd; he couldn't decide whether she was a child or a woman. She walked over to a tall young man who had so many muscles that he must get tired carrying them around. The man had blue eyes and floppy yellow hair and—

Hold everything, Wayne. When he reached Winnemucca the score hadn't been thirty-one to nothing. It had been thirty to one. This guy had whisked by them in a convertible, back about fifty miles on U.S. 40. What had fooled him was that the convertible's top had been up and anyway police didn't ride around in convertibles. That showed how wrong you could get. Because Deputy Sheriff Carson Smith did ride around in a convertible. He had ridden in one all the way from Cheyenne to Winnemucca, and probably not just to swim in the pool of the Sonoma Inn.

Smith and Holly sat at a table under one of the striped umbrellas, and began talking earnestly. Bill watched them for a moment. For all he knew, Smith was asking pointed questions about the activities of a guy named Wayne. He walked quietly up behind them and heard Smith saying, "Hope you don't mind my saying so, ma'am, but you shore look purty."

"Why, thank you," Holly said in a fluttery voice.

"Yes ma'am," Smith said. "Mighty purty."

For some reason this irritated him more than if Smith had been trying a murder charge on him for size. "Try a little variety in that," he said. "Make it purty as a picture."

Smith swung around. "Oh, here's that Wayne," he growled. "Just keep on like that, and you and me will—"

"I was just lending you a few words. You seemed to be running the same ones over and over."

Smith started to get up. "This here range," he said, "is too small for you and me."

The guy had muscles like a wild stallion. It was a shame to waste all that power on an ordinary guy named Wayne. "You're not in Cheyenne any more," Bill said. "Don't get too tough with me."

"What would you do to stop me?"

Bill smiled pleasantly. "I'd call a cop."

"Will you please quit this?" Holly said. "You two are like a couple of first-graders pushing each other around at recess."

"He's bigger than I am," Bill said. "I think he's a ringer from the third grade. But if he'll lay off, I will."

"I'm right sorry we annoyed you, ma'am," Smith told Holly. "I'll try to see it don't happen no more."

Bill said, "What are you doing here, anyway? I don't think you'll find many rustlers camped at this waterhole."

"Oh, I'm just riding around," Smith said.

Just riding around, eight hundred miles from Cheyenne. The guy was about as mysterious as a cop stomping around on his beat. Ten to one, it had something to do with the murder in Cheyenne. If he needled Smith carefully the guy might blurt out something worth hearing. "I thought you had a murder case to play with back in Cheyenne," he said. "Did you solve that, or just get bored with it?"

"Well, it ain't exactly solved…"

"But pretty nearly, huh? All but finding out who did

it and catching him? I get it. You came here so the murderer back in Cheyenne wouldn't suspect you were chasing him."

"What do you think I am, dumb?" Smith said angrily. "He don't happen to be back in Cheyenne. He drilled another feller last night in Salt Lake City and I figger he's moving west and—" He stopped suddenly, looking worried. "I hadn't ought to say things like that," he muttered.

Holly said, "Don't feel badly. Bill was to blame. He shouldn't have teased you into saying it. We'll all forget the whole thing."

"Mighty kind of you, ma'am," Smith said. He glared at Bill and said, "I want to make sure that goes for you too, Wayne."

"As far as I'm concerned, you just came here for a swim."

"Come to think of it," Smith said, "you could say I'm taking a few days off. Matter of fact I am. The sheriff don't think much of the idea I'm working on so I told him this was on my own. If I could break this case I figger I could beat out the sheriff, come next election."

"I wish I could vote for you," Holly said softly.

"Mighty kind of you, ma'am. Well, like the feller said, I just come here for a swim. Care to join me, ma'am?"

"You go ahead," Holly said, "I'll join you in a moment."

Smith nodded, and sauntered to the edge of the diving board. For a moment he posed there magnificently, as if a sculptor had asked him to be the model for a work to be titled "The Hero." Probably an ordinary sculptor couldn't do justice to him, though. It would take somebody like Gutzon Borglum, who had a spare mountainside. Bill watched without any pleasure. There was a rumor that cowboys couldn't swim and he hoped it was true. Smith gave a spring and did a perfect jackknife and sliced neatly into the water. He popped up and began churning up and down the pool. It looked as though he had a small outboard motor attached to his feet.

"Beautiful to watch, isn't it?" Holly asked.

"Any fish can do better," Bill said. "Most of them can probably out-think him, too."

"You aren't doing very well at thinking. I simply cannot understand why you go out of your way to irritate him. It isn't safe."

"I don't agree. The more he dislikes me as a person, the less chance he'll think of me as a possible suspect. Would any normal suspect go out of his way to needle a cop? No. Besides, I like to needle him."

"You're being childish."

"You told me once that you played up to the guy in Cheyenne to irritate me into giving you a little attention. You were certainly playing up to him just now, before you knew I was around. How does that add up?"

"It's quite simple, Bill. I wanted to find out why he

was here. If I play up to him, I bet I can find out anything I want."

"The question in my mind is, what do you want to find out from him? That you're mighty purty?"

"Yes," she said coldly. "I'm beginning to think I do." She left him and plunged into the pool.

He sat for a minute watching them act like seals at play. He was getting a little mixed up in his mind about the girl. Of course he didn't want her tagging along after him. But for some reason he didn't want her tagging along after Smith, no matter how good her motives might be. He got up and went back into the hotel. There was no use taking a swim now. Compared to Carson Smith, he would look like a man struggling to reach a life preserver.

When he went to the dining room later on he saw them at a table for two in the corner. Holly was certainly putting on quite an act for Smith…if it still was an act. She wouldn't be the first girl who put on an act for a big handsome guy and then found she wanted to keep playing it indefinitely. He joined some of the other tourists at a larger table. He studied the menu and ordered some things he disliked and ate them.

Smith and Holly had a leisurely dinner and finally strolled into the bright little casino next to the dining room. He followed as far as the doorway and leaned against it, watching. Smith bought some chips and went to the roulette table and began playing. In half an hour he had hit the house for ten bucks or so, and Holly was cheering him on as if he had struck Mother Lode.

Finally Holly excused herself and came past where he was lounging and beckoned for him to follow. She paused in the hallway and said angrily, "The way you act, if there had been a crime around here, people would think you were returning to the scene of it."

"I'm just an admiring audience, is all."

"Not with that look on your face. Don't you realize Carson will get suspicious of the way you watch him?"

"He isn't very bright. Tell him I'm madly in love with you and that I'm jealous."

Her face turned red. "I see your point," she said. "Naturally only a very stupid person could believe a thing like that was possible. But Carson isn't as stupid as you think. I've had a lot of trouble coaxing him to talk about the murder."

"Sure. He wants to talk about you. Has he worked up to saying you're cute as a button?"

"It just happens that I *have* learned a few things. Carson found a scrap of paper in that man's garage in Cheyenne. It was in the murdered man's handwriting and carried some figures. Up at the top it said: 'Me—$9,870.' Below that, in a column, it said: 'Ken, $3,150. Frankie, $820. Cappy, $1,900. Domenic, $5,300.' Then the figures were added up and a lot of angry-looking question marks put down at the end. What do you think of that?"

"Put down a lot of scared-looking question marks for me."

"Can't you guess what it means?"

"I can guess what it meant to Russ. Those must be the amounts each of the gang has chipped in, so far, toward buying up the lake where the plane sank. What worries me is what Smith figured it meant."

"I told you he isn't stupid. He decided those amounts were big enough to indicate a pretty interesting deal, and that maybe one of the men on the list might know something about the murder."

Bill muttered, "Then I suppose he found an address book Russ kept, and identified all of them."

"No. There wasn't any address book. In fact, Carson said the desk in the garage looked as if it had been looted by the murderer."

"That's possible. I was unconscious for maybe twenty minutes. Cappy or Domenic might have taken the address book and letters they'd written and the map of that lake. By the way, the list knocks out that mystery man you were dreaming up. Only five names on it."

"I suppose you're right. Well, anyway, Carson asked around town, and at the place where Russ boarded. He picked up a fact here and there, and found that Russ had known a man named Ken in Salt Lake City and one named Frankie in Reno and a Domenic somebody in Los Angeles and a man named Cappy in San Francisco. No last names. No addresses. He decided to make a trip and see if he could locate the one in Salt Lake City or the one in Reno. The sheriff didn't want any part of it and said he was crazy."

"He's my favorite sheriff."

"So Carson drove to Salt Lake City. He arrived last night and went to a tourist court and when he got up this morning and looked at a newspaper what do you suppose?"

"Yeah. A guy named Ken killed in about the same way Russ had been. How much has he told the cops in Salt Lake City and his boss in Cheyenne?"

"He didn't tell them anything. He decided Ken was the first man on his list and that he'd better get to Reno fast and try to locate the second. He wants to solve the case himself and get all the credit. What do you think we ought to do?"

"I ought to give him Frankie's address in Reno and save time. With his luck, he'll probably yell 'Hey, Frankie,' on the main street of Reno and Frankie Banta will come up and say, 'You calling me?' "

"Oh, stop it!" she said. "You're always getting discouraged."

"What can I do? If I can get to Frankie before Smith does, maybe I can coax him to talk. Always assuming I'm right in thinking Frankie isn't the killer. I don't know any better plan."

She said thoughtfully, "If you started tonight—"

"It's a hundred and sixty miles. How do I get there, steal Smith's convertible?"

"No, I guess you couldn't. And besides in an hour or so he'd discover it was gone."

"Oh, would he? Is he planning to take a little

drive tonight? With somebody I know, maybe?"

"Well," Holly said, getting pink again, "he's been asking me and asking me and I've been trying to refuse but—"

"If you're serious about not wanting to go, I'll let the air out of his tires."

"Your mind is always wandering off on detours! Just remember this is a serious business. I believe I *will* go for a drive with him tonight. And I'll coax him to make a date to show me Reno tomorrow night. That ought to slow him down."

He tilted an eyebrow at her. "Slow him down?"

She said furiously, "I'm talking about slowing down his murder investigation!"

"There used to be a famous old picture. It showed people in a sleigh throwing out a baby to slow down a pack of wolves. This is a modern version of it. Except that in this case, baby is jumping out all by herself."

"I can take care of myself. I've been around."

"You've been around the first grade. You're playing with the big boys now."

"Oh, I don't know," she said coldly. "Only one of them seems to be big. If you'll excuse me I'll go back and join him."

He watched her march into the casino. Carson Smith had a manhunt and a woman-hunt under way, and he seemed to be making progress on each. It was annoying, Bill thought, not to be able to decide which hunt was giving him more worries.

Ten

This was Reno. It was filled with people trying to hit jackpots on slot machines and hoping to break the bank at roulette and blackjack and faro. Compared to a character named Bill Wayne, they were betting on sure things. First he had to find Frankie Banta, which was beginning to look like one chance in a hundred. Then he had to convince Frankie he hadn't killed Russ and Ken, which was one in a thousand. Finally he had to coax Frankie to spill everything. One chance in a million.

The other people in Reno were merely gambling with money, and if they lost they could go back to Woonsocket or Wichita or Wenatchee and make some more. He was gambling with time: five minutes here, ten there. Any moment he might dig down for more and find he had just lost his last second.

It was ten at night and he had been hunting Frankie for almost seven hours. At eight the next morning, the Treasure Trip bus would roll west, heading for Yosemite National Park. He didn't like the idea of staying behind to play a lone game; he would have been sunk back in Salt Lake City if Holly hadn't saved him. But staying behind when the bus left was a minor worry. His major worry was that things seemed to happen fast to his former pals as soon as he hit town. Frankie Banta might be running short of time, too.

The bus had reached Reno early that afternoon. As soon as the party checked in at a tourist court, he slipped away and started hunting for Frankie. The address he had was a rooming house and it was a dud. Frankie had been kicked out months earlier for dropping behind in his rent. Five bucks bought another address from the landlady, but five bucks didn't go far in Reno and the address was no good. He went back and bought a better address for ten bucks. This one was all right but Frankie wasn't in his room. The second landlady said Frankie was a bellhop at one of the hotels but she wasn't sure which. He did pick up one useful fact: the landlady said Frankie hadn't been out of town in all the time she had known him. So that cleared Frankie of the murders.

He went paging the guy at the Mapes and Riverside and finally, long after dinnertime, found he was employed at one of the smaller hotels. Oh no, he wasn't there. You didn't hit jackpots that easily. Frankie was off duty.

For ten bucks the bell captain had some ideas. "It's like this, mister," he said. "Frankie is slot machine silly. All he does in his spare time is play them. That is, he plays them when he has some dough. When he doesn't, he goes around making notes on how different machines pay off. Always trying to find a machine he can beat. He keeps saying he's gotta make a stake. I never could figure what for. He don't have a dame or anything."

No, Frankie didn't have a dame. Frankie was in love with a chunk of gold at the bottom of a lake somewhere in the mountains. Some of his friends were going to bust up that romance, if Frankie didn't chip in his share toward buying the land around the lake. "Doesn't he ever win?" Bill asked.

"Well, you know the percentages. They cut you to ribbons. He hit a thousand-dollar jackpot once, but what happened to it I don't know. He was as broke as ever the next week."

There had been a list in Russ Nordhoff's garage in Cheyenne. On it was the note: Frankie, $820. That was what happened to it. "Is he playing or watching tonight? And do you know where?"

"He had a few bucks. So I guess he's playing. But he could be anywhere in town."

Anywhere meant a corner drug store or a restaurant or Harold's Club or a hotel or anywhere. Slot machines were all over the place. There were enough of them in town so you could play two at a time if you liked the idea, and a lot of people did. They fed one machine and pulled the lever and fed the other and pulled its lever and looked to see what the first had done and fed it and pulled its lever and looked to see what the second had done and so on. That way you didn't lose any time, only money. He wished he knew a way not to lose any time.

He went from place to place and his head got dizzy with the sound of silver dollars chinking and levers clacking and croupiers droning and girl attendants calling jackpots. Those sounds didn't leave him much chance to listen for really important noises. Like, for example, the tap of footsteps following him down Virginia Street. Or the rustle of somebody trailing him through the crowds in one of the big gambling joints. Maybe he wouldn't have heard any noises like that even if there had been no chinking and clacking and droning. Maybe nobody was trailing him. And maybe nobody was waiting, somewhere near Frankie, for Bill Wayne to come along and take the rap for another killing. Maybe not. He didn't want to bet on it, though.

He walked among the joints looking for Frankie. You had to look carefully because most of the faces seemed as blank and similar as if they had been stamped out like silver dollars. For example, there was a guy with dull blue eyes who didn't look quite as human as the machine he was playing. He—

His heart gave an odd whirring quiver like a machine getting ready to pay off.

"Hello, Frankie," he said quietly. As he spoke he shoved a hand into a pocket and made like a gun. "Just take it easy," he said. "Don't start yelling how glad you are to see me."

Frankie was thin and pale and his hairline was backing away from his forehead. He didn't move. He stood there and watched the wheels of the machine click to a stop. Two plums and an orange. Nothing came out of the machine. A little sweat came out of Frankie.

With his free hand Bill brought out a quarter and put it in the slot. Frankie's hand came up mechanically, jerked the lever. Two cherries and an orange. Five quarters clattered cheerily into the cup. "See," Bill said, "I'm bringing luck."

"I knew it must be you," Frankie said, in a voice with no more ring in it than a lead quarter.

"That's interesting, Frankie. What does it mean?"

"I'm talking about Cheyenne and Salt Lake City."

"You have some ideas about what happened there?"

"Look, Bill, I don't want to get you sore. But maybe you're sore enough already so what I say don't matter. Yeah, I got ideas. I can read the papers, can't I?"

"All right. You read about Russ and Ken. Why do you add that up and get me? Did you even know I was alive and back in the States?"

Frankie's hand reached slowly into the cup of the machine and collected the five quarters and put one in the slot. "You probably won't believe this," he muttered. "I never wanted you shot. In my book you were a good guy. I wasn't the best radio operator in the world but you always gave me a break. I didn't know you would get shot and I felt bad when you bought that slug in the back. I'm the only guy in the bunch knew it didn't kill you. All of us was gathered around where you was lying and I got down and felt under you. I could feel your heart sort of fluttering and yet it wasn't pumping out any big stream of blood and I figured you had a chance. I said you was dead and let's get the hell out of there. I thought that might give you a break, like you used to give me. You don't have to buy this."

"I might put a down payment on it for a few minutes. Keep playing the machine, will you? It looks better that way."

Frankie hauled down the lever. Two cherries and a lemon. Three quarters rattled down. Frankie began feeding them slowly back into the machine as he talked. "So I figured you might pull through and get back here some day."

"Nobody told you I was back?"

"In this bunch of ours," Frankie said, "nobody gives out nothing for free. If any of the others knew, they didn't tell me." He gave the handle an angry yank. The wheels spun and stopped on a collection of fruit salad.

"You think I shot Russ and Ken?"

"Who else could have?"

"You guys don't waste much love on each other. What's wrong with somebody else in the bunch knocking off Russ and Ken?"

"Look, Bill," Frankie said in a tired voice. "I ain't blaming you. They had it coming to them. But none of the others did it for two reasons. The first is we been back in the States for over four years. If anybody in the bunch had wanted to knock off any of the rest, that's a long time to wait. The second reason ought to give you a laugh. None of the others would have started by knocking off Russ and Ken. They'd have chopped me down first."

"I wouldn't want to make you feel bad, Frankie. But you don't look that dangerous to me."

"So I'm not dangerous. But I'm a drag on them, see? The bunch of us have a big deal on. We're each supposed to ante up a lot of coin. I don't ever make any real coin. I make a little and feed it into these machines trying to latch onto some big money and end up bumming a buck for breakfast. The other guys in our bunch get pretty sore at me for not coming across. If anybody knocked me off they'd give him a medal."

"This is the lake deal you're talking about?"

"You know about it, huh? You got it out of Russ or Ken?"

"Yeah. If you figured you were next on my list, why didn't you skip town?"

Frankie gave a laugh that blended perfectly with the clack and clank of slot machine levers. "Skip to where?" he said. "On what? I come here tonight with six bucks and I owe everybody around Reno I could borrow from. And if I do skip, so what? You're still looking for me. And maybe the other guys start looking for me. They'd figure if I'm scared enough to run I'm scared enough to talk. I'm tired. I'm ready to quit. What are you fixing to do, take me for a walk somewhere?"

He studied Frankie's thin profile. The guy looked as if he had been feeding his blood as well as his money into the machines. Maybe he could take a chance with Frankie. "You know what I have in this pocket next to you?" he asked.

A quiet shudder went through Frankie. "Sure. A gun."

"It's a hand with five fingers on it. That's all. Take a look." He pulled out the hand and extended it, palm up.

Frankie looked at the hand like a kid trying to figure how a magician had done a trick. "I don't get it," he said.

"I don't have a gun on me. I didn't come to Reno to take a shot at you."

A little color seeped back into the thin face. "Ain't you taking a chance on me, Bill?"

"I have to take a chance on somebody. I need help."

"Like maybe to find that lake up in Oregon and a few other things?"

"Yeah. And a few other things."

Frankie began to laugh. He jammed a quarter into the machine and yanked the lever and hit three oranges. "This is getting to be my lucky night," he said, scooping up a handful of silver. "I was trying you out on that one, Bill. That lake ain't in Oregon. You don't really know where it is, huh? I see why you're taking a chance on me. I see why you need help. Listen, you came to the right guy."

"You may be the right guy but you have some wrong ideas. It's like this, Frankie—"

"I get it, I get it," Frankie said impatiently. His face was fever-pink and his hands trembled as he yanked away at the lever. "The two of us can do business, see? You can't trust none of the others and I don't blame you. And none of the others would trust you. But you can trust me, see? And I know you're a good Joe. We each got something the other hasn't. You have guts, see? You can handle the others. I can tell you where the lake is and everything else. And we split fifty-fifty. Right?"

All the guy could see was a slot machine that was ready to pay off. You put a little information in the slot and pulled the lever and out came half a million bucks. "It doesn't work like that, Frankie. The deal is—"

"I'll listen to reason," Frankie said in a whining tone. "Okay, you get fifty-five and I get forty-five."

"The forty-five you'll get is a bullet."

Frankie jerked. "Don't scare a guy like that!"

"It's time you got scared. I didn't kill Russ and Ken."

Frankie played several quarters slowly and frowned when none of the right combinations hit. "Could you prove it?"

"No. And if you get knocked off I probably won't be in the clear, either. But it will be somebody else doing the job, all the same. One of the others has turned killer. I've got to find out which."

"This is where I came in," Frankie said disgustedly.

"We went over this before. I told you why I can't go for it. Why would the guy have waited years to start shooting? Why didn't he start on me?"

"Because he didn't have an alibi until I came back. Because he had to have a stooge he could blame it on. He didn't start on you because you weren't the first one on my visiting list. Now do you see?"

"Sure. Sure, Bill, anything you say."

"You don't believe me, though."

"You tell me what to believe and I'll believe it."

Frankie's mind worked in one groove, like a slot machine lever. "I need some questions answered," Bill said.

"First the deal."

Bill said angrily, "Don't be so dumb! The deal is you don't get killed."

The color in Frankie's face had gathered in two burning patches on his cheekbones. He was feeding the machine and yanking the lever viciously and not even looking to see if anything came out. Nothing did, though. "I might just as well be dead," he snarled. "What kind of life have I got? Toting luggage for quarter tips. This window don't work, boy. Get me some ice water, boy. What's good for a hangover, boy? I'll buy any story you want to peddle. I don't care who knocked off Russ and Ken. If it was somebody else he saved you trouble. All I want is to be cut in on the deal and cut in right. It's the only chance I have, see? Make me a good offer and I'm your boy. Don't make it and the hell with you. All I want is your word, see? Do we do business?"

All Frankie thought of was the big jackpot. And what Frankie didn't see was that the percentages were against him worse than they were on the slot machines. Frankie was betting his life on this gamble and the percentages said he didn't look healthy.

Bill shrugged and said, "Okay. We do business. You can have half of what's coming to me."

"That's great!" Frankie cried. "We'll be a team, Bill. We—"

"Give me one answer right now, will you? Who was the guy who shot me?"

"Good old Bill," Frankie said, chuckling. "The answer to that is gonna surprise you. Let's go somewhere and have some food and talk. You know what? We made this deal just in time. Here's my last quarter." He put it in the slot and yanked the handle and watched the wheels click into place. "Lemons," he said, and gave the handle a final disgusted yank.

Something paid off on that yank. It paid off in a crash of sound that kicked in your eardrums. Frankie lurched forward. He grabbed the slot machine and for a second hung there, face blank, clinging to the machine as if he were in love with it. Then he slid down it like wax on a candle and melted into a quiet heap on the floor.

An object came through the air in a lazy arc and hit Frankie's body and clattered against the machine. A big gray automatic. Bill stared at it and thought numbly: guess whose?

It seemed like an age before he snapped out of the coma. Probably it was only a split-second, though, because everything else around him was moving slowly too. For instance a girl way down the line of machines past Frankie was opening her mouth to scream and Bill had time to spot the gun as a forty-five and figure it was his before the girl's shriek jabbed his ears. He jerked around to see where the shot had come from. Nobody stood behind him. Nothing was there except a row of slot machines. One of them was tired of being mauled by Frankie and had shot him in the back with three lemons.

Wait a minute, Wayne. Walk, do not run, to the nearest insane asylum.

The rows of machines were double, with each machine backed up against another. Between each set of back-to-back machines was a space of several inches. Somebody had lounged behind that double row of machines and reached into the opening and aimed the forty-five and waited until Frankie's back came into line and let him have it and then flipped the gun through the opening so a guy named Bill Wayne could claim it. What would you bet the killer used a glove or handkerchief to avoid fingerprints?

Right after the roar of the shot faded there hadn't been a sound. Then the girl's scream cracked the silence and now a wave of sound was cresting. He couldn't think in all that racket. Anyway what good was thinking? He bent and grabbed the forty-five and yanked the slide and saw a fat cartridge tumble out. Thanks for leaving me some, bud. He ran fast, jaw set, eyes glaring, down the row and around the end. Now he could see down the aisle where the killer was. He crouched, balancing on his toes. Come on, Domenic. Come on, Cappy. Come and get it.

Signals off. Try thinking again, Wayne. That guy trying to dig a foxhole in the floor isn't Domenic. The one trying to climb over the machines to get away isn't Cappy. If either of them was there, he was hidden in that traffic jam down at the far end of the aisle. Nobody wants to meet you, Wayne.

The big curving double stairway to the ground floor was right behind him. He waved the gun at a couple of men who were sneaking in on him from the side and watched them go over backward like pins in a bowling alley. He turned and started down the stairs. Before making the turn that would bring him into view of the first-floor crowd he jammed the gun in a pocket. He rattled around the curve in the staircase and saw a polka-dot pattern of faces staring up at him and heard a bell begin clanging like mad.

He stopped, screamed at them, "Up there! Up there, quick!" He pointed up at the second floor.

Four guys charged out of the crowd below and went up the stairs two at a time past him, yanking at things in hip pockets. The crowd yelled. Ordinary guys with nothing but wallets and handkerchiefs in their hip pockets caught the fever and rushed up the stairs too. Behind him the place went crazy. Guys charging up the stairs crashed into guys charging down. It looked as if somebody had pulled the lever on a slot machine as big as a house and the thing had paid off with a tumble of angry men.

He was going to be unpopular when they sorted out that mess. He ran down the rest of the way and burrowed through the crowd and had almost reached the door when people on the stairway began pointing down at him and yelling stop that guy he's a killer. Right away the people in front of him wished they were the people in back of him. A lane opened up as if he were following an invisible bulldozer and he raced through it and out the doorway.

He sprinted down the street toward the nearest corner. Nobody was in his way. Nobody was on the sidewalk at all. Not ahead of him, that is. Behind him they were pouring out into the street and setting up the long wild howl of a crowd with something to chase. He darted around the corner and raced down the next block and above the thump of blood in his head heard the clatter of footsteps gaining on him. This wouldn't last long. He made the corner and turned it and flung himself into a doorway just around the corner. He shucked off the coat, stuffed the gun inside, dropped it. Three men pounded around the corner and past him before they saw the street was empty. He leaped out and ran into them as they stopped.

"There he goes!" he yelled. "Down that alley!"

When a mob got started it didn't take much to keep it going. The three men sprinted ahead blindly toward the alley and other men boiled around the corner and followed. Bill kept up with the leaders for a few paces and then gradually lagged and let some of the others pull ahead. This was working out all right. When two more men passed him he would stop with a painful stitch in the side. Maybe nobody would be able to identify him now as the man who had fled from the gambling club. Most people didn't have photographic memories: a face flashes past them and they get the sort of fuzzy snapshot a kid takes with his first box camera. As soon as two more men passed he might be safe.

Atta boy, there goes one: a nice clean-living youngster with a good pair of lungs and the stride of a miler. Number Two was right behind his own shoulder. Number Two wasn't passing him very fast, though. Probably out of condition, didn't take good care of himself. He slowed to give Number Two a chance. Number Two was playing out, however. A hollow shell of a guy. Number Two's footsteps kept pace with his own slowing ones. He didn't want to glance over his shoulder. Looking back in a chase like this was a suspicious move. But he couldn't help it. He looked back.

About that hollow shell stuff—how wrong can a guy be? This was nature's gift to the wide open spaces. Running easily, right behind his shoulder, was Deputy Sheriff Carson Smith. And there was a look on Smith's face that made you think of a prairie wolf running down a lone calf.

Eleven

For a moment he panicked. He put his head down and sprinted. The pavement started sliding by under his feet in a smooth blur and a couple of the figures running ahead of him got larger. The quick hard rasp of footsteps just behind him kept pace. He couldn't shake off the sound. He tried to sprint faster. That didn't work. His head was jerking up as he strained for air and his knees were pumping too high. The blur of the sidewalk broke up into jumpy streaks.

He glanced back again. Smith was loping along easily. You could almost imagine him lolling out a big red tongue and showing long teeth and grinning like a wolf at the end of a chase.

"Looks like yore playing out on me, pardner," Smith called.

That was the clincher. The guy was not only keeping up with him but also had enough spare breath to get talkative. He himself didn't have enough spare breath to blow out a match. It would be nice if he had, because a lot of matches seemed to be flaring up inside his chest. He stopped. A lot of men went pounding past him, but Smith stopped too, and lounged against a wall watching him fight for air.

He managed finally to get a breath of air that wasn't filled with smoke and sparks, and gasped, "What are you waiting for?"

"Just bein' sociable," Smith said blandly. "Thought I might jog along with you some more when you got your breath."

That wasn't what he had expected. When he asked what Smith was waiting for, he was thinking in terms of handcuffs. Maybe he had been wrong. Perhaps Smith didn't know he was the man everybody was chasing. Smith might not have seen him come rocketing out of the gambling club. Smith might not know there had been another killing. And the guy couldn't know that the dead man was named Frankie and was the person both of them had come to Reno to find. There were a lot of mights and perhaps and maybes in that. Against them you had to weigh the wolf grin that kept twitching Carson Smith's mouth. When you put everything on the scales the balance was dangerously even. Maybe—here comes another maybe—Smith wasn't quite sure of the exact score and was waiting for him to make a move that would confirm his suspicions. If so—yeah, let's try an if for a change—this would take careful handling.

"You have plenty of wind left," he said. "I haven't. Maybe you can catch the guy."

"What would I do with this feller if I caught him?"

"Run him in. Arrest him. What do you think?"

"I don't know what to think," Smith said. "Lot of

fellers come rootin' and tootin' by me and I come along to see the fun. What would this feller have done?"

Was this on the level? He didn't want to bet on it. "I was playing the slot machines in a club on Virginia Street and some guy ran out with a lot of people screaming after him. Maybe he pulled a holdup."

"This here's a no-good town to pull a holdup in. Ain't but a few roads out of Reno. What with mountains and deserts they're right easy to block off. Feller won't get out of town."

"You might grab some credit if you caught him."

"Shucks, I don't know," Smith said. His coat fell open as he lounged against the wall of a building and the star on his left breast pocket winked. Next to it something else winked from a shoulder holster. "Don't hardly seem right to come into another man's corral and rustle off one of his killings."

The night air began making ice cubes on his sweating skin. He said hoarsely. "Why are you talking about a killing? Don't you mean a holdup?"

"Did I say a killing? Shore, a holdup. But now rein in there, pardner. Didn't I hear a couple fellers yelling it was a killing as I come by them? Can't rightly recollect. But if I did hear fellers say that, it could have stuck in my head. But you say it was just a holdup?"

Getting words out was like pulling fish hooks up his throat. "I was taking a guess. It could have been a killing. It could have been a holdup. Or both. How do I know?"

"Shore, shore," Smith said soothingly. "I figgered mebbe you knowed the answer on account of you was way up there in the bunch chasing the feller when I caught sight of you. Wasn't you right on the feller's heels at one time?"

That grin was on Smith's face again. You read about wolves circling a herd and making little dashes forward hoping to start a stampede. Was Smith playing that game or was he just dumb? "I don't think I was in the lead," he mumbled. "There were always a few ahead of me."

"You get a good look at this feller, Wayne?"

"Dark trousers, no hat, a coat flapping open, that's all."

"A coat is a mighty handy thing in this country at night. It can chill off right fast. You ought to wear a coat, Wayne. Shirt of yours is sopping wet. Man can catch his death of cold or something."

Or something. Why did he throw that in? "You're probably right," he said. "Maybe I'd better get inside somewhere."

"You don't want to do that yet awhile, pardner. You got to take it slow, like cooling out a horse by walking him after he gets all lathered up. Come on. I'll walk you around a piece."

This added up like a wolf worrying over whether a sheep has enough wool on to keep warm. He didn't know what he could do about it, though. He started walking slowly down the street with Smith beside him.

The chase had flooded far past, leaving driftwood patches of men who had given up. Some of them were talking about whether or not the leaders had caught the fleeing man.

"Shucks," Smith said. "I don't reckon they'll catch nothing. These city fellers don't know the first thing about a chase. You ever tracked a coyote, Wayne? A smart coyote will double back on his trail so fast you'll get dizzy watching him. I bet me and you have as good a chance of running into that feller anywhere along here as the fellers up front have of catching him. You figger you'd spot this feller if you seen him, Wayne?"

"I might."

"No use moseyin' along nowhere while you get cooled out. Tell you what. I've chased a lot of coyotes. Just for fun let's me and you figger where this coyote might have gone, and see can we walk him down. He might have doubled back into a doorway right after turning that corner way back there. Then after some of the fellers ran by he could have chased along with the rest of the pack and right about here he could have figgered it was safe to turn off. How does that listen to you?"

That was pretty accurate, except for the part about turning off here. He tried to study the expression on Smith's face, but the broad-brimmed hat threw deep harsh shadows on it and all he could see was a gun-metal glint of eyes. "It sounds like nonsense."

"Well, let's find out," Smith said cheerily, gripping his arm and swinging him into the side street.

That made Smith ninety-nine percent right. The hunted man *had* turned off there. The thing on which Smith was one percent wrong was that the hunted man didn't figure it was safe. But if Smith was suspicious, the only chance he had was to go along with him, acting innocent. It began to look as if he had underrated the guy right from the start. It now seemed possible that Smith used his head for other purposes than as a hitching post for a Stetson.

They walked down the side street, and in a couple of blocks Smith made another guess about where the hunted man had gone and they turned up another street. It was very quiet out here. Houses were getting farther apart and no lights gleamed in them. The sound of Smith's boot heels echoed hollowly, as if they were walking inside a giant empty barrel. The sound blended with the tap of blood in his head until it felt like a tiny hammer striking his skull. "Just a little piece more. University of Nevada campus is up here this way. Reckon it's a lively place with the boys around. Kinda dead now."

Kinda dead. The campus and Bill Wayne had a lot in common.

"You know what?" Smith said. "I run out of the makings. You got some tailor-mades on you, Wayne?"

His cigarettes and matches were in his coat, back in that doorway. "No," he said. "I don't have any."

"That's a funny thing. Most times I seen you, you been smoking."

"I just don't happen to have any."

"Funny thing, ain't it?" Smith said. "Well, we come quite a piece. You figger that feller might have come all the way up here?"

Bill took a deep breath that went down his wind-pipe like an icicle. He didn't like the sound of Smith's question. He hadn't liked any sounds from the moment he heard the thump of Smith's feet running behind him, but this was the worst. If Smith enjoyed using that gun in his shoulder holster he would never get a better chance. Deputy Sheriff Kills Gunman in Marathon Chase. Maybe Smith hadn't been suspicious at all. Maybe he had been sure right from the start. A fast way to find out was to make a break for it. He didn't like that way.

"Well, what about it?" Smith said, grinning. "Do you figger he came up here?"

Bill set his feet, got ready to move fast. "Yeah," he said. "I think he did."

That jolted the guy. It knocked the grinning mask off his face and left a snarl. That did it. Bill started a right hook. He put his shoulder and body and toes into it. It slammed into the big square jaw and sent sparks whipping up his arm. Smith lurched backward, clawing at his shoulder holster, wide open for more hooks. Bill threw them into him, short jarring hooks into face and ribs and stomach. This was good. This was great. He liked this. Smith crashed back against a tree and sagged there and Bill planted himself solidly and let go big crazy swings and watched Smith come forward in a slow toppling fall.

He stared at the man on the ground. His hands ached and he was breathing hard but he felt good. He had actually taken the guy: a tribute to good clean living and getting in the first fifty punches. Smith had been so anxious to use the gun that he had forgotten he could have won the brawl with his fists.

He knelt and examined the guy. Smith was not going to be reaching for his gun within the next few minutes. But when he did, it might be nice if he had to hunt for it. Bill reached into the shoulder holster and dragged it out. He broke it open, shucked out the cartridges, threw them in one direction and the revolver in another. Then, just to be safe, he patted Smith's pockets. It turned out he was Two-Gun Smith. His hip pocket carried an enormous bulge. Bill pulled out the weapon, looked at it, shivered. It was his .45 automatic. Smith must have seen him coming out of that doorway where he had dropped his coat, and had paused long enough to grab the coat and find the .45 and bring it along. Smith had certainly planned to have the case all wrapped up. He didn't seem to have overlooked any angles except that a sock on the jaw is worth two guns in the holster.

He stuck the .45 under his belt and covered it with his shirt and started back toward the center of town. In one way the fight had left him keyed up and slightly drunk. In another way it had left him with a hangover. Actually he wasn't much better off than before, except that he was still alive. He was in favor of staying alive but probably a lot of people would vote against it. He had three problems.

The first was Carson Smith. Fortunately Smith wasn't likely to go to the Reno cops with his story; if the story got out he would never live it down. But Smith did know where to start looking for him. It would be very unsafe for him to rejoin Treasure Trip of the Old West or even try to pick up his things at the tourist court.

The second problem was the Reno cops. They might or might not have a good description of him. They would be combing the town and setting up road blocks at the outskirts. A lone man wandering around town, or trying to check in at a hotel or tourist court, might arouse suspicion. He had to find a place to hide until morning.

His third problem was the guy who had shot Frankie Banta. Only two of the crowd were left now: Cappy Judd and Domenic Ferrante. One of them was in Reno and had done the job. It was possible that the guy named Wayne had outlived his usefulness and had been promoted to number one on the hit parade. It was also possible that he could be useful in taking the rap for one more murder.

He was interested in staying useful for a while. And

besides, finding Cappy or Domenic and making one of
them talk was his only hope of clearing up the mess.
So what he had to do was hide until morning and then
grab the first bus to Frisco. The prospects of getting
away safely on the bus didn't look good. On the other
hand, if he tried to stay around Reno he wasn't likely
to last as long as a divorce hearing in Washoe County
Courthouse.

He walked south until he found a bridge over the
Truckee River, and threw the .45 upstream. According
to tradition, the girls threw their wedding rings into
the Truckee after getting their decrees. If they did, no
doubt some canny citizens made a business of fishing
out the rings and might find the .45 and wonder if one
of the girls had been too impatient to wait for a
divorce. But frankly, he didn't believe the tradition.
Women were practical about jewelry; if they threw
anything into the river it was probably something they
got for box tops. Anyway the .45 had a dull gray finish
and might be mistaken for a rock. Anyway he had no
choice.

There were, he remembered, a couple of park areas
downriver which might be good places to hide until
morning. He headed that way. He had almost reached
the first one when he saw a car combing the park with
a spotlight. Well, he hadn't really wanted to spend a
lonely night in a park, anyway. Maybe he could mingle
with the crowds downtown and walk around until he
thought up a better idea. He turned north and then

east and arrived back on Virginia Street, where some of the biggest gambling clubs were located.

Before you can mingle with a crowd, Wayne, you have to find a crowd.

Virginia Street was deserted. The Biggest Little Town in the World looked as lively as a Sunday School on Saturday night. Of course the answer was easy. Everybody was inside the clubs. As he passed lighted entrances he saw crowds hanging over gambling games, as sober and intent as surgeons around an operation. He wandered aimlessly, trying to decide what to do. Once he passed the doorway where he had hidden to let the leaders of the mob chase by. His coat was still there. He emptied the pockets and dropped it in a sidewalk trash container. Let the cops make something out of that if they could. Let—

Speaking of cops, here comes a prowl car. The boys may feel lonely with nobody on the streets and be looking for company.

A doorway threw a welcome mat of light across the sidewalk in front of him. He walked through the doorway and found himself in one of the big clubs. If he wanted a crowd to hide in, here it was. And maybe this was the last place where anybody would look for him. Of course he would have to face the hideout problem all over again when the club closed.

He stopped an attendant and asked, "How late do you stay open?"

"How late? We don't ever close."

"You mean people are gambling here all the time?"

"Sure. Five in the morning. Seven. Right around the clock. You don't even have to go out to eat. If you want some sandwiches or anything just speak up."

Or anything, huh? It would be nice if he could order a new face, preferably one not as plain and certainly not as well-known as the one he was wearing. He began the long dull process of killing time until morning. Gambling with money looked tame compared to what he was doing. He wandered from one game to another, making a small bet now and then to pretend he was interested.

He was feeding nickels slowly into a slot machine when somebody paused beside him and said acidly, "I hope you get lemons."

He jerked around and saw Holly.

Twelve

The girl's face was pale. There were lavender smudges under her eyes and her ponytail of bright hair was drooping and she looked as if she had been kept up far beyond her bedtime. He glanced around to see if anybody he knew, such as Carson Smith, had been keeping her up. She was alone, though. This was a new problem. Perhaps she didn't know about the night's events. He hoped she didn't; she was in this too deeply already, and he wanted her to go away and forget she had seen him.

She said, "That was a mean trick, sneaking away the minute we reached Reno. And without a word to me, either."

"Teacher," he said wearily, "I don't have to attend your classes. I've passed the truant officer stage."

"Yes, you've worked up to real policemen, haven't you? Did you find that man?"

"Who, Frankie? I missed him."

"Oh, did you?" she said in a grim tone. "Well, somebody didn't."

She knew, all right. "I wish you'd beat it and forget you saw me."

"That wouldn't do you any good. Too many people remember they saw you tonight."

"Have the cops got a good description of me?"

"No description of you could be very good. But they certainly must have some interesting ones. According to one I heard, you're seven feet tall and have red eyes and came running down the stairway after the murder waving a knife in each hand. Another person claimed you were five feet six inches tall and had a scar that twisted the left side of your face into a snarl. Then a silly impressionable woman told me you're almost six feet tall, handsome in a tough sort of way, black hair, dark eyes, heavy dark eyebrows that have a slanted rakish look. That's quite close, except for the handsome part."

"Where did you find out all this?"

"Why, it's all over town! How could I miss?"

"Did any of the Treasure Trippers happen to be in that place and see me come running out?"

"None that I've talked to."

"Do the cops know my name?"

"I wouldn't know," she said coldly. "They haven't taken me into their confidence. Nobody has."

"And you don't know which description the cops are betting on?"

"No. But I wouldn't want to be a man seven feet tall, or one who is five feet six with a scarred face, or one who looks like you, and try to get out of town. Or stay in town, for that matter."

"You have a real knack for cheering me up."

"Your best chance is to hope none of our crowd saw you, and leave with us as if nothing had happened. In a crowd you may get through."

"It won't work," he said. "Your glamor boy knows. I refer to Side-Saddle Smith."

"Oh no, Bill!"

"Oh yes. He chased me down and marched me to a deserted part of town and was going to shoot me and run for sheriff."

Her gray eyes looked big and shocked. "But you're alive and here! I don't understand."

"I knocked him out. I don't understand either."

"I simply can't believe it. He's so big and strong and—"

"He's just the most wonderful guy in the world," Bill said irritably. "But he wasted so much time counting the notches on his gun that I managed to leave a few notches on his jaw."

"You'd better tell me the whole story."

"All right. But you'll have trouble believing it too."

She listened to the mistake-by-mistake account of his evening, and then said, "Is that the whole story? Is that really it, from beginning to end?"

"No. That's just from beginning to now. Stick around a few hours and maybe you'll see the end."

"I'll have to think what to do."

"On Fridays I do my own thinking. This is now Friday. What you can do for me is scram."

"You won't last twelve hours by yourself. Look at you now, right out in the open where anybody can find you."

"This is the best place in town to hide."

"Is it? I had no trouble finding you."

"You have an advantage. You knew I like hiding in crowds. You knew I signed up for the Treasure Trip so I'd have a crowd to hide in. Wasn't that the way you figured tonight?"

"Well, yes. But you're doing a very bad job of acting like one of this crowd. You don't show any interest in gambling. You play these machines like a man forking over his income tax. You haven't put in a nickel while we've been talking. That girl attendant has been watching and is starting to wonder about us. Put something in, will you?"

He dug into his pocket and brought out a coin and tried to fit it into the slot of the nickel machine. The coin was a quarter and wouldn't go in. He moved down the line a few machines and dropped it in a quarter machine and pulled the lever. "You can't help me the least little bit," he said. "Please go away and—"

"Look!" she cried.

"Are you crazy, yelling that way? You—"

"Jackpot!" she screamed.

Bill turned and gave the machine a dazed look and saw the three bars lined up. He reached in his pocket for another coin to get rid of the things but just then the girl attendant brushed him aside and looked at the machine and called in a loud clear voice, "Jackpot! Number four hundred and twenty-six!"

Several people turned to look at him. He whispered to Holly, "See what you did! Everybody's looking. If you hadn't yelled I could have slipped another quarter in the slot and wiped that thing off."

"That girl was watching," Holly whispered. "She would have known something was wrong if you tried to get rid of a jackpot. Besides it's five hundred dollars! You can use it."

"No," he muttered. "I never liked elaborate funerals. I—" Somebody tapped him on the shoulder. He turned, ready to go quietly, but it was a man in a neat dark blue suit who smiled at him and said, "Congratulations, sir. That is the four hundred and twenty-sixth jackpot made here since eight o'clock yesterday morning. You have won five hundred dollars. Would you like it in cash?"

He was still groggy from that tap on the shoulder. "Make it a check," he mumbled. "Payable to William—"

Holly stabbed him with an elbow, and said quickly, "Cash would be better. Can we have it in twenties?"

"Certainly," the man said. He brought out a wallet and counted a sheaf of currency into Bill's hand. "Good luck," he said, and walked away.

Bill shoved the money into a pocket. People were still looking at him enviously, and he started to move to another part of the club. Somebody else tapped him on the shoulder; they might just as well shoot him as keep on doing that. This time it was the girl attendant.

She said, "Wouldn't you like to put in a coin and remove the jackpot from this machine? It's customary. Of course we will do it, if you prefer."

He was sick of this. "I don't have a quarter left," he growled. The sooner he could get to another part of the building, where people weren't watching him, the better. Holly said, "Here's one," and gave it to him. He scowled at her and put it in the machine and yanked the lever and walked away. Suddenly Holly began screaming on a rising pitch, like an air raid siren. He whirled. Holly and the girl attendant were staring at the machine. The girl attendant straightened up, blinking, and called in a shaky voice, "Jackpot! Number four hundred and twenty-seven!"

He walked back to them on legs that had turned into old broomstraws. "It must be a mistake," he said thickly.

The man in the neat dark blue suit rushed up and said, "What are you trying to pull? You got paid for that one. Don't try that stuff around here."

Holly cried indignantly, "He isn't pulling a thing! All he did was hit two jackpots in a row."

"I saw it," the girl attendant said. "I don't believe it but I saw it."

"You're in it with them, are you?" the man said.

People were starting to crowd around, chattering. A heavy man in a checked shirt shouted, "I saw the guy put in the quarter and pull the handle. He hit that jackpot. Don't let them shove you around, mister."

The man attendant stuck out his jaw and said, "These machines don't hit twice in a row."

"They do too!" a woman cried. "I saw a dollar machine hit twice in a row one night in Harold's Club. Did they squawk? No."

The man in the checked shirt grabbed Bill's arm and said, "Make 'em pay, mister. I'll run out and get you a cop."

Bill stared at him dumbly. The room was a big cement mixer whirling faces and voices around him. A cop would be swell. Pardon me, officer, but I came in here to hide out from a murder rap and these crooks won't pay off. "I don't want any trouble," he muttered. "Let's forget the whole thing and—"

The protesting howl of the crowd drowned his words. A big man in a sharply creased gray suit brushed through the crowd and snapped a few questions and then said to Bill, "Sorry this happened. Hope you'll accept the apologies of the house." He turned to the man attendant and said, "Pay him," and walked off.

The attendant took a deep, counting-to-ten breath and recited, "Congratulations, sir. That is the four hundred and twenty-seventh jackpot made here since eight o'clock yesterday morning. You have won—" another quivering breath "—five hundred dollars. Would you like it in cash?"

The crowd laughed and cheered. "Yes, cash, please," Holly said.

The man counted out the money slowly and then went up to the machine and put a hammerlock on it and wrenched it around as if he were wringing a neck. He said, "This machine is out of service," and stood with his back to it, arms folded, glaring at Bill.

Bill shuffled guiltily away. He found Holly clinging to his arm, and he whispered, "What will you take to beat it?"

"Me?" she gasped. "Look at the luck I brought you!"

"Next time try bringing good luck. Half the people in the place are watching us."

"Don't be silly. This is perfect. Haven't you ever watched a magician at work? He does something very obviously with one hand to catch your attention while he does the trick quietly with the other. It's called misdirection. You caught everybody's attention by hitting two jackpots in a row and nobody would think you were trying to hide."

"If a magician gets a big enough audience, somebody in it will know how he does the trick. And baby, we got an audience."

In fact it was a little difficult to move away from that haunted machine. People kept patting him on the back and urging him to stop and try some of the other machines. A big man in a checked shirt—the one who had offered to call the cops for him—blocked the aisle and protested, "You can't walk off like this, mister.

You're hot. I've seen it happen before. You can take this place apart. Just put a couple coins in. Come on. Just for fun."

"No," Bill said.

"Then be a sport and stick this one in for me." The guy forced a silver dollar into his hand and grabbed his arm and hauled him to a machine. "How about this one?" he said eagerly.

This was crazy. Still, all he had to do was hit a few lemons and that would get rid of people. He pretended to study the machine carefully and then shook his head and muttered, "No. Not this one." He moved to the next dollar machine and put in the man's coin and yanked the lever. The wheels spun. Click. An orange snapped into place. Thank heaven for that. He couldn't have taken another Bell Fruit Bar. Click. Another orange. Now wait a minute, machine. Take it easy. Take—click. Another orange. He shuddered as eighteen silver dollars rattled down into the cup.

The crowd roared. It was ridiculous. He had seen crowds act this way at a prize fight when the underdog suddenly began clouting the champ all around the ring. Only this time he was in the ring. He was the underdog, the way people always were against gambling machines, and he was clipping the champ. They loved it.

Holly put her lips close to his ear and whispered, "There's no use trying to walk out. People will follow you all over town. And you simply can't stop playing. It will look queer. Find something to play where you won't create such a riot."

"This is your riot."

"Try roulette, Bill. That's a quieter game."

He shoved through the crowd toward one of the roulette tables. It was crowded but word of what he had done was spreading and somebody got up and gave him a stool. He changed some money into chips and began playing blindly. He wasn't quite sure what he was doing, but nobody was screaming "Jackpot" now so probably things had cooled off. As time went on he noted with relief that his stacks of chips didn't seem to get much bigger. Something odd had happened to the color of them, though.

He looked around and saw Holly next to him and said, "I thought I started with white chips. Now they're all blue. How come?"

Her eyes were as big and round as the chips. She swallowed once, said huskily, "If you *will* keep on winning, what can you expect?"

"Am I still winning?" he said in a horrified whisper.

"The white chips were dollar ones. The blue chips are twenty dollars. What do you think? And on top of that I've been taking chips away and cashing them in whenever your stacks began to get too big."

He peered over his shoulder, and shivered. Behind him rows of faces were stacked up like eggs in a crate. He said, "How much have I won?"

"I—I don't know, Bill. My handbag is jammed with

money. It's…it's sort of horrible, isn't it?"

"Hah!" he said bitterly. "I haven't been winning since I hit town. Don't let this fool you." He slapped a blue chip on number 30, which was the age they would inscribe on his tombstone, and watched the wheel stop with the little ball cuddled in number 30. The croupier's hand flicked in front of him and went away leaving a couple more stacks of chips.

"Bill," Holly said faintly, "I'm going to leave for a little while. Do you mind?"

She was running out on him. He didn't blame her a bit. "Good luck," he muttered. "Buy yourself a hair ribbon with that money."

"I'll—I'll be back."

Sure, she would be back, and snake eyes was a lucky number to roll in craps. What was the use of feeling bad about it; he'd wanted her to clear out, hadn't he? He took a final look at her as she slipped away through the crowd. She wasn't a bad kid. Probably she'd make a nice partner for a guy who didn't mind repeating first grade the rest of his life.

He turned back to the roulette table and tried to concentrate on what was happening. It was very diffi-cult. The moment he got things sorted out, the croupier would spin the wheel and the red and black numbers and faces and chips and lights would all mix together in a rainbow blur. He knew he was winning, though. Piles of chips teetered higher and higher in front of him and faces around the table stacked up like chips. An attendant moved in beside him and cleared a space and set up a special table for his chips. It was absurd. All that money and he couldn't make carfare out of town.

Time went by and finally he noted something interesting. He had stopped winning. The stacks of chips were shrinking. The stacks of faces were shrinking. The table vanished from beside him. After a long time he ran out of chips. He looked around. There weren't many people left, and they were no longer paying attention to him. He stretched rusty joints, looked at his watch. It was five in the morning.

He grinned at the croupier and said, "We had quite a hassle."

The croupier had a face like boiled dumplings. "I only worked part of the time, Mac. You wore out the other guy. Usually it don't make no difference to us, win or lose, but something about the way you played rattled the other guy."

"How much was I ahead?"

"I wouldn't want to say, Mac. Might make you feel bad."

The guy was wrong there. He didn't feel badly at all. What they didn't realize was that he had come off a winner. He had won quite a few hours, and a few extra hours of life were worth any amount of money you could name. Unfortunately, winning time left you with a gambler's urge to win more, and he wasn't quite sure how to do it. He got up and walked unsteadily toward the rear. He passed a row of slot machines and stopped to search his pockets and found a silver dollar and dropped it in a machine. The wheels clicked around. Lemons. That was the last of his money.

Somebody caught up to him and asked, "Did that break you?"

He stared at the guy through a haze and recognized the big man in the sharply creased gray suit who had settled the jackpot argument, hours ago. The gray suit looked rumpled now. "Yeah," he said, "that was it."

"What about that girl who was with you earlier? She took away a good hunk of change. She didn't come back. Think she will?"

He grinned. "Do they ever come back?"

"Well, I guess you're right. What are you going to do now?"

"I thought I'd wash up and then try to figure what to do."

"No place to stay?"

"No. But that's all right. You don't have to worry about me."

"Come up to my office," the man said. "You can catch a nap up there. Then you can shower and shave and I'll have breakfast sent up. I wouldn't want you to go out like this. I'll be honest. It would give me a bad name. You put up a swell show. Drew the biggest crowd I've had in a year. A spending crowd, too. I made out all right."

He had just gambled a dollar and won a few more

hours. "That's mighty nice of you," he muttered. He followed the man to a private office and sank down on a leather couch.

"By the way," the man said, looking slightly embarrassed, "I hope you didn't mind those pictures."

"What pictures?"

"Well, I had a photographer take some shots and rush them over to the newspaper. Good publicity, see? Reno visitor wins seventy-six thousand bucks. I'll be honest. I can't have them running a follow-up saying you walked out broke."

"I had seventy-six thousand dollars?"

"All of that. You won it nice and lost it nice. I like a man can do that."

"Will that picture be in the local paper?"

"Yeah. I didn't try to get your name to send in with it, though. Sometimes that can embarrass a winner. Well, catch yourself a good rest up here and I'll stake you to wherever you're heading."

Bill nodded weakly. When that picture got out people were likely to identify him as the man hunted for the murder earlier in the evening. He refused to get excited about it, though. He was so tired he couldn't make it out of town now if the guy had offered to stake him to an armored car. "Thanks," he mumbled, and went to sleep.

Thirteen

Somebody was shaking him. It was a dull faraway feeling and he lay quietly hoping it would stop, as an alarm clock will stop if you have patience. Whoever was shaking him had a self-winding attachment, however, and kept right on. Finally he opened his eyes. Things spun in front of them for a moment like the wheels of a slot machine, then settled click-click-click into place: ceiling, walls, pictures, desk, a face. All these objects belonged to the man who ran the joint.

He looked at the man and said, "Sorry to take so long waking up. Sometimes a lighted match under my toes will do the trick faster."

"I'd have tried that," the man said, chuckling, "except you had your shoes on. How do you feel?"

"I'll live," he said automatically. Then he wondered if, considering everything, that might not be too optimistic.

"Good. Catch yourself a shower if you want. Right in through that door beside my desk. And I left out a razor and things. Breakfast will be ready out here for you when you finish. I'll be back in a little while."

Bill thanked him and went into the bathroom and took off his clothes. When he unstrapped his wrist watch he saw it had stopped. He shaved and dressed and went into the office and found a waiter setting the table. He asked what time it was. It was eleven A.M. He sat down and ate breakfast irritably. He felt the way a lot of people do before they have their morning coffee. He felt the same way after he had his morning coffee. He had no plans and no interest in making any. He smoked a cigarette made of old shredded boot heels and watched the door open and the owner of the joint come in.

The guy said, "Well, I have a stake for you."

"Thanks a lot. You've been swell. I don't want you to stake me, though."

The man grinned and said, "I don't think you'll object."

Through the doorway came Holly Clark. She looked as young and excited as if she were about to graduate from high school.

The owner of the joint said, "They do come back sometimes," and went out.

"Hello, Bill," she said gaily. "How are you this morning?"

He stared at her. Seeing her took a big load off his shoulders. It took the load off his shoulders and dropped it into the pit of his stomach, where it made him feel sick. He was positively not going to analyze his feelings toward this girl to see if she meant a lot to him. He had no right to have any feelings about her except an urge to get her out of this mess and keep her out. "How am I this morning?" he repeated. "I'm sane, thank you. I needn't ask how you are. You're crazy."

"Did you think I would walk off and leave you?"

"I figured you would be smart and run, not walk. Am I right in thinking it's eleven in the morning?"

"Eleven twenty-one."

"And the bus left at eight?"

"Yes. Bill, do you realize that I carried away nine thousand four hundred and twenty dollars of your winnings in my handbag? Aren't you pleased?"

"I sure am. We can hire a good lawyer for you. I hope they have some in Reno who work on criminal cases instead of just divorces."

She said in a low voice, "Let's not do a lot of talking now. We might be overheard. I'll tell you everything later. Are you ready to leave?"

"Do we bow pleasantly to the cops or snub them as we breeze out of town?"

"Be quiet and come on!"

She really was taking his hand. She was linking her fingers confidently in his hand and walking him arm-in-arm downstairs, peeking up happily into his face every few steps. The owner of the joint was at the doorway. The guy said "Good luck" and then they were crossing the sidewalk and Holly was opening the door of a car with long borzoi lines and white sidewall tires and discreet gleams of chromium and enough red leather upholstery to equip a high-class bar.

"It's yours. I mean, it's in my name because

someone had to sign the papers but I bought it with your money. Four thousand eight hundred and fifty dollars. It's only six months old. Like it?"

"You're bats," he said. "You even have the top down. I'd just as soon try to make a getaway in a diamond-studded bathtub. Everybody will be looking."

"Exactly. Just as they were looking at you last night and seeing a lucky gambler instead of a man on the run. It's that same business of a magician catching your attention with one hand while he does the trick with the other. Please get in."

He shrugged, and slid behind the wheel. Rows of dials and gadgets gleamed at him from an instrument panel that could probably handle a B-29. "How do you start this yacht?"

"You put a little pressure on the accelerator pedal and turn the ignition key. Then you move the lever from N, which means neutral, into D, which means drive. R is for reverse and L is for—"

"You don't have to spell it out like c-a-t," he said irritably.

"Turn right, please." She kept giving him directions until they reached one of the parks along the river. Nobody was around, and she suggested stopping. "Now," she said, "I suppose you want to know the score."

"I already know the score. We're losing badly. All I want to know is how to call time out."

"Would you like to see your picture in the paper?"

She reached to the back seat and brought out a newspaper and showed it to him. There he was in two columns on the front page, sitting groggily beside skyscraper piles of chips. Fenced off from his picture by a very thin column rule was a big story headlined: BLOCK ROADS, SEARCH TOWN, FOR MURDERER. Think of the trouble they could have saved by knocking out that column rule and extending the headline over his picture.

"It's not a very good likeness," Holly said.

"Let's protest to the editor."

"I mean, in a way that's lucky. I'm not sure that most people could recognize you unless they looked at you and at the picture together."

"Let's make it easy for them. Let's buy an expensive convertible and put down the top and ride around attracting attention."

"Oh, but we want people to recognize you as we drive out of town."

"This is getting a bit complicated for me," he muttered. "Let's start with something easy. Such as, why are you here instead of a hundred miles away in California?"

She drew her legs up onto the seat and hugged her knees and took a deep happy breath, as if getting ready to tell him one of those stories that begin once-upon-a-time. "When I left you early this morning," she said, "I took a taxi back to the tourist court. I meant to get your baggage and hide it where we could pick it up today. But I couldn't."

"What's that in the back seat?"

"That's your baggage."

"Good. That straightens me out. Please go on."

"You see, Carson Smith was prowling around the tourist court. Of course he was looking for you but he pretended he had been looking for me. I was supposed to have a date with him last night but I was out looking for you."

"Smith pretended he didn't know what had happened?"

"That's right. So after a while, to get rid of him, I said good night and went to my cottage. But he still hung around in the shadows. So I couldn't do a thing. There he was this morning when everybody was getting ready to leave and I didn't dare sneak away so I started off on the bus with the others. They were all asking about you but none of them connected you with that murder. So I pretended to be getting more and more worried about you and finally, just as we reached the last gas station in Reno on the way west, I had the bus stop and I got off with your baggage. I told everybody I thought it was my duty to make sure you weren't sick or hurt in the hospital. I said I'd catch up with them in Yosemite. The bus driver can handle things while I'm away."

"Then you got a taxi back to the center of town and

went to an auto dealer and bought the Queen Mary and had them put wheels on it."

"It's a lovely car, isn't it? We're going to drive to Yosemite. There's a back way. We go south from here and then enter the park from the east over Tioga Pass. It's nine thousand, nine hundred and forty-one feet high. I understand it's quite a tricky road and it's only open a few months a year and the buses don't dare use it. But that route is much shorter than the way our bus is going, and we can get to Yosemite Valley late this afternoon before our bus does."

"Then I rejoin the tour and if Carson Smith shows up I tell him he can't tag me because I'm on home base?"

"Oh, stop worrying so far ahead. We aren't even out of Reno yet. Isn't that enough of a worry for you?"

"No. I've had that one so long I'm getting sick of it."

"Our Miss Clark will handle the matter," she said cheerfully, starting to get out of the car. "Just sit there and bite your nails quietly." She went to the rear of the car and lifted the lid of the luggage compartment and busied herself with something mysterious. Then she came back and gave him a very odd smile. For some reason her face was bright pink. "I don't think you're going to like this," she said, and tossed a handful of rice and confetti all over the car. "We're pretending we were just married."

You might think the girl had suddenly gone out of her mind, but actually she had not been in it lately.

"Now I've had it," he said. "When you decide to break the camel's back, you don't bother with a last straw. You use a haystack."

He got out of the car and walked around to the rear. She had festooned the rear bumpers with white paper streamers. He didn't know how she had restrained herself from scrawling a JUST MARRIED sign. He marched back to where she was standing. She faced him regally, chin tilted, gray eyes clear and scornful. In some way she managed to give the impression that he was a small and grubby boy whom she had caught throwing spitballs in her classroom.

"Well?" she said.

What she did was bad enough, but her attitude made him want to burn down her school. "You win," he said. "But you're going to have to live up to this. Let's see how you like it."

He grabbed her wrists and shoved them behind her back and jerked her up close. She gasped, tried to pull away. He locked both wrists in his right hand and slid his left hand up her back and laced his fingers through the soft ponytail of hair. It made a nice handle. It let him force her head into exactly the right position. Not that he was going to kiss her. He was merely going to hold her locked this way, with her mouth a fraction of an inch from his, and let her sweat it out for a minute. Then maybe she would realize that girls who played with fire sometimes came out done to a turn.

Her breath came in warm puffs and her body

quivered all along his like a flame. There was really
no use doing this halfway. Her mouth crumpled softly
against his and her trapped body moved in little deli-
cious attempts to get away. Her heart seemed to be
clanging like a big gong against his chest. That ought
to teach her a lesson. He released her, stepped back.
He had been wrong about that gong effect. It was
inside his own chest.

Holly covered her face with her hands and climbed
blindly into the car.

"I see you don't like living up to it," he said.

She took her hands down and said, spacing out the
words like slaps in the face, "I don't like living down
to it."

"Isn't that a shame? I always kiss the bride. Especially
my own."

He climbed in the car and started the engine. Holly
stared straight ahead, giving him curt directions where
to turn. They came out on U.S. 395 heading south and
drove about a mile and suddenly he saw the State cops.
Their car was parked a hundred yards ahead and one of
the cops was in the middle of the road signaling a stop.
Bill stretched out an arm and swept Holly close to him.

She tried to pull away, and he said, "Cops ahead.
We got married, not divorced, remember?"

"I-I forgot. I was so busy thinking about—Bill, I'm
scared. Let's turn around. I may give us away by
showing how scared I am."

"Lots of brides get scared. The cops will think it's

that. Here we go." He stopped the car beside the State trooper.

"License, please," the trooper said, watching him carefully.

He got out his wallet and handed over the license. The trooper took it in his left hand, keeping his right free, and gave it a glance. Up ahead the trooper's partner lounged beside the police car, a hand resting on the butt of his revolver.

"Owner's card, please," the trooper said.

"You have that, Holly," Bill said casually.

She had been sitting beside him as rigidly as a totem pole. She moved perkily and opened her handbag and brought out the license.

"You just bought this car?" the trooper asked.

Bill waited for Holly to say something, but apparently she couldn't. She didn't realize that the time to get scared had been hours ago, when she was skipping around a murder case as if it were a Maypole. "My girl bought it this morning," he said. Then he chuckled and added, "I don't mean my girl. I mean my wife. We were married this morning, too."

The trooper looked at the confetti and rice. He started to grin, then switched to a slight frown. "Hey, Arch," he called to his partner. "Come here. These two say they just got married."

The second trooper walked toward them, and Bill wondered if one of the pair would ask to see the marriage license. That would wreck things.

The first trooper said to his partner, "What do you think? Anything familiar about this guy? What about that description?"

"I guess you saw today's paper," Bill said. "Man, was I all over it! Look here." He reached to the back seat and grabbed the newspaper and spread it out for them to see.

The first trooper looked at it. He studied the photo, showed it to his partner. You could see him relax: a beautiful sight, like sunset over the Pacific or a baby's first smile. The trooper whistled softly. "You won all that?" he asked.

"They tell me I was seventy-six thousand bucks ahead at one time. But I didn't know. And of course I didn't hang onto it either. But my girl was smart and sneaked away with about ten thousand while I was playing and didn't know the difference. So that staked us to this car and getting married. Wonderful car, huh?"

"Wonderful car?" the second trooper said. "Look, Mac, you mean wonderful girl."

"It's a gorgeous car, though," the first trooper said wistfully. "Do you think we could catch a job like this if we had to chase it, Arch?"

"I wouldn't bet on it," the second trooper said. Then he looked at Holly and said, "You look worried. Is anything wrong?"

Holly tried to speak a few times and finally gasped, "I'm scared about being married," and huddled against Bill and began to cry.

The first trooper put a hand up to his face and tried to smooth away a grin. "You'll be all right," he said soothingly. He leaned close to Bill and whispered, "Lots of them get like that. The kid I married, hell, I almost had to drag her down from the ceiling." Then he straightened and said in a normal tone. "Here are your licenses. Good luck. Take care of this swell car."

"Take care of that swell girl, too," the second trooper said, still voting for love over horsepower.

"Thanks," Bill said. He shoved the licenses in his pocket and waved and sent the car sedately down U.S. 395.

Holly remained crumpled against him for about a mile. Finally she lifted a tear-streaked face and said, "I'm so ashamed. I wasn't a bit of help. And I almost ruined things."

"Ruined things? That was the perfect touch you added."

"But I didn't even think of it myself. It was something you said, and it just happened to pop out at the right moment."

"Remind me to take you along when I want to rob a bank," he said. "I'll send you in first, weeping, to say you're afraid your savings aren't safe. The bank staff will spread out every nickel in the joint to console you, and then I'll walk in and scoop it up."

"I don't think I'm a good criminal."

"I'd hate to see you get any better. You just engineered the perfect getaway. I owe you an apology for sneering at your plan."

"You owe me an apology for something else, too."

"If you're talking about the way I grabbed you, I did it because I disliked that just-married gag. I wanted to teach you a lesson."

"You enjoyed doing it," she said accusingly.

"I wouldn't want to insult you by saying it was a chore."

"I do not need to be taught any more lessons."

He grinned at her. "Okay. School dismissed."

"Very well," she said primly. "And now I think I will take a nap."

Holly awoke as they finished the thirty-mile run to Carson City, and informed him that it was the smallest capital city in the United States and that she would like a sandwich and coffee. After a brief stop they headed south again. Holly wasn't feeling talkative and the halt in Carson City had for some reason shattered his peace-pipe mood. Besides, he saw a gray sedan in the rear-view mirror. It seemed to adjust its speed to his. Of course that wasn't unusual; on long drives lots of people tended to let the car ahead set the pace. He didn't want company, though. He nudged the accelerator and heard the kittens under the hood grow up into cats. The convertible streaked down the deserted road, banking nicely on turns and whooshing up the rises as if begging him to ease back on the wheel and take off.

Holly didn't like so much speed, and said so. She pointed out that, while the Nevada law didn't set an exact upper limit, it used the term "reasonable and proper." She had odd ideas about danger. Apparently she thought the speed of a bullet was reasonable and proper but eighty miles an hour in a car wasn't. He didn't slow down. It was too hard to shake off that gray sedan. Miles went by before the mirror no longer showed it coming around a distant curve.

They zoomed down a grade and leveled off beside a blue lake and flicked past a California boundary sign, and then he had to clamp on the brakes for a plant inspection station. Two other cars were ahead of him and the wait would give the gray sedan time to catch up. He waited, sweating a little, while the other cars were inspected. The gray sedan didn't arrive. He hadn't wanted it to catch up, but he wasn't happy about the fact that it refused to catch up when it had a chance. He peered back, trying to see if it was parked far back on the road, waiting. The road looked empty.

The plant inspector reached them finally and asked if they had any plants or vegetables or fruit. He looked into the luggage compartment.

Bill asked, "What do you do if you find stuff like that?"

"We confiscate it," the inspector said. "It might be carrying insects or diseases that could damage California crops."

"You're going to have fun with a car behind us."

"What exactly do you mean?"

"Oh, we got to talking to some people at a gas station up the road a way and—"

Holly asked, "What *are* you talking about?"

"Let's not cover up for them, honey," Bill said. "You know they'd been collecting desert plants all through Nevada. After all, it is against the law to bring that stuff into California." He turned back to the inspector and said, "It's a gray sedan. They'll be along any time. They may have their plants hidden."

"Thanks a lot," the man said. "We're good at finding stuff."

Bill waved and pulled out from the inspection station and sent the car whisking down the road. Just as he took the first turn he thought the rear-view mirror showed a glitter of chromium and a gray hood slipping into sight far back.

"Remember me?" Holly said. "I'm in this with you. If you don't tell me what's happening I'm likely to break our necks tripping over one of your little schemes. A gray sedan is trailing us, is it?"

"It probably doesn't mean anything."

"You went to a lot of trouble to delay him at the inspection station. That sounds as if you're taking him seriously."

"Well, he's probably just an ordinary tourist. But he got on my nerves by sticking too close after we left Carson City."

"He didn't catch you, though. You don't think it's the police?"

"When I first noticed him I wasn't going fast and he could have caught me easily. So he's not a cop chasing us. In fact I don't think it's anybody important to me at all."

"You mean important to us."

"Let's get this straight," Bill said. "You're not in this with me. You're an innocent bystander. You don't know a thing about any of these murders."

"That will be news to the police."

"You can make it stick. Last night you bumped into me at that gambling club. You had no idea I was dodging a murder rap. I started to win a lot of money gambling. Then I told you that a couple of guys I'd known in China were in town, looking for me with guns on account of something that happened over there. I gave you a hunk of money and told you to buy a big fast car and bring it around to the club so I could get away safely. I told you not to breathe a word of it to anybody. I said if you were a good kid and did what I asked we'd get married before we left. You'd been falling for me, see?"

"This is beginning to sound like a fate worse than jail."

"You didn't really want to buy a car and run off with me. You went back to the tourist court hoping I'd show up before the bus left. But when I didn't you couldn't ride away with all that money. You got off the bus and then decided to get me the car. You brought it around and I talked you into getting married."

"It was quite a ceremony. Just the two of us. No minister."

"There was a justice of the peace," he said sharply. "A fake one. You didn't know that. You didn't realize until afterward that I must have hired some hanger-on at the club to pretend to be one. We picked him up at a place he claimed was his home and drove around while he pretended to marry us. I explained I was too worried about my ex-pals from China to wait around in a house. He signed a hunk of paper and gave it to us and we dropped him off. Later when you came out of the rosy glow and asked to see the marriage license, you suspected it was a phony, and then I laughed and tore it up."

"Do you really think I could get away with that story?"

"Sure. Just tell it with a lot of tears. How can they prove anything? And don't forget that I'll back you up if necessary."

"If necessary and if alive. That story makes me look like an awful idiot."

"Would you rather look like an idiot and walk out free, or look like a smart girl in jail?"

"You're not giving me a very wide choice."

"There isn't any choice, if the cops ever grab you. But there's a good chance you may never be dragged into it. Now have you got the story?"

"I've got it," she said, "but I'm not sure I'm going to keep it."

"Holly, if you—"

"Let me think about it for a while, will you? Don't rush me."

About an hour after leaving the plant inspection station they reached the turn-off to Yosemite and swung west and saw the Sierras banking up ahead of them like cumulus clouds.

He whistled and said, "Maybe I should have brought my airplane."

"It's hard to believe a road actually goes through those mountains, isn't it? Bill, I've finished thinking about your scheme for keeping me out of trouble."

"You didn't find any holes it, did you?"

"Well, for one thing, that story wouldn't sound very convincing unless I left you when we reached Yosemite."

"Of course it wouldn't. I can't rejoin the party and you can't stay with me."

"What are you planning to do?"

"Buzz down to Frisco and L.A., hunting for Cappy and Domenic."

She took a deep breath and said, "I don't think you're going to like this. I want to go with you. Now don't scream too quickly. I can help, honest I can. You need somebody to keep looking behind while you're looking ahead. You need somebody to play scout and ask innocent questions and warn you if somebody's

following or spying on you. I can do all that. And
you've got to have help. You'll never get out of this
mess if you don't. You—"

He had been holding back the explosion as long as
possible but now it ripped loose. He told her how
many kinds of an idiot she was. He explained the riski-
ness of her plan in words of one syllable that she might
be able to understand. He said she would be about as
helpful as a broken leg. She sat curled up on the seat
and watched him with hurt eyes.

When he ran out of breath, she said plaintively, "I
thought about your plan and now you ought to think
about mine."

"Yours isn't a plan. It's a suicide pact."

"But will you think about it? For a few minutes?
Without arguing or—"

The future caught up with him that second. It
caught up in a roar of horsepower and yowl of tires.
One moment the road behind was empty and the next
moment a car whipped around a hairpin turn back of
him and came zooming up like a fighter plane making
a pass. The road had just made a switchback that put
him on the outside. His brain flashed a warning: crazy
driver, pull over, give him room. He swung the big car
close to the low guard wall, close to the drop into blue
space.

Then he got the word. It came awfully late. He was
the crazy driver, not the other guy. Roaring up on his

left on the inside of the road came the gray sedan with one guy crouched behind the wheel and another glaring out at him. Hello, Cappy. Hello, Domenic. This is it, huh? The gray sedan slammed in at him and he braced for the crash.

Fourteen

Fenders hit like ash cans falling downstairs. Next to him Holly screamed. He jammed the accelerator down to kick the car from high into third. A surge of power came roaring from the big engine and his body jerked back with the pickup. The convertible leaped forward, crowding into the gray sedan and forcing it to straighten. They rocketed forward together.

The narrowness of the road had blocked the sedan from cutting into them from a sharp angle. But for that, they would already be over the low guard wall and spinning into space. Up ahead was the payoff. Up ahead the road hooked left and the wall swept across his course and over the wall loomed miles of sky. If he didn't get to that turn first he'd need wings. He gripped the wheel and stood on the accelerator. He gained an inch. Two inches. A foot. He was almost even with the sedan. His car had more weight and power. But it was jammed against the sedan and helping carry it along. The turn was racing toward him. He had to gamble. He gave the wheel a twitch to the right and broke clear for a second and felt the car lunge ahead and then spun the wheel hard left and slashed across the road.

That was it. He had a three-foot lead and a quarter-ton in weight and fifty extra horses under the hood. The sedan swerved, vanished in a clang of metal on rock as if a giant hand had brushed it off him. He didn't have time to look back. That hairpin turn was on his neck and he was jolting the car with quick jabs at the brake and hearing the tires skid and catch and skid and watching blue sky wheel madly past the hood and then feeling the last skidding lurch and seeing the wonderful empty road straightening ahead.

He took a deep slow breath. "You know what?" he said. "A guy can get his fenders dented that way."

Holly looked at him with solemn eyes. "I thought people only got into dogfights in planes, not cars."

"That's the disappointed fighter pilot in me. What happened to him? Did you see?"

"You ran him into the side of the cliff and his rear skidded around and he almost turned over and finally stopped broadside across the road."

"Did he start up again?"

"I don't know, Bill. About that time you began doing barrel rolls and loops and a few other things they taught you in the Air Force. Was it my imagination, or at one time were we actually out in the wild blue yonder?"

"Some driving, huh? I didn't know I could do it either. You don't look as scared as you ought to be."

"If you would like me to break down and have hysterics it will be no trouble at all."

"You're doing all right. Better than I am. That chattering you hear is not from the valves but from my knees knocking."

"It was deliberate, wasn't it, Bill? They were trying to knock us down that awful drop?"

"Just a couple of old pals playing tag. Pals by the name of Cappy Judd and Domenic Ferrante. Hang on for a minute, will you? I want a little more mountain between our car and theirs."

He concentrated on driving for a few minutes, taking turns at a speed just short of a skid and roaring up the straighter grades. Finally he braked to a stop on a level stretch and yanked back the emergency. The motor was still running and the car sat in the middle of the road so that nobody could pass. He jumped out.

He made a quick check of the left side of the car. It would make some repair shop very happy. Nothing serious, though. He looked back down the road, listened. Not a sound. He walked to the guard wall and leaned over it and peered down the steep tumble of rock. The road zigzagged below him like a fire escape and far down he saw a gray car with a couple of tiny figures pushing and hauling at a front wheel. He couldn't resist a temptation. He picked up a chunk of rock and threw it. The rock went curving down and for a pleasant moment he pictured it bashing in one of their heads. The line was right but the slant of the mountain wasn't. The rock dropped short, went bounding down with a little stampede of other rocks following it.

One of the tiny figures looked up, crouched. Bill grabbed another rock. His arm started the throw and then not far above his head the air made a snapping noise and up the mountain came the rattling echo of a shot. He made a wild pitch and jumped back into the car and got going.

"That must have been fun," Holly said. "If you met a rattlesnake would you insist on biting it out with him?"

"Taking a shot at me was a mistake on his part. When he thinks about it he'll be glad he didn't hit me."

"Aren't you being too charitable?"

"Look at it this way. I'm no good to Cappy and Domenic with a bullet hole through me. That is, not unless they can hide the body where it won't be found. They want to fix things so I take the blame for three murders. So I either have to vanish or get knocked off in what looks like an accident."

"You certainly have logic on your side. I wish you had a little self-restraint, too."

"Yeah, well, I admit I lost my head there too. I can't afford to knock them off. They're my only chance of clearing myself. I've got to get one of them alone and beat the story out of him and then call in the cops and pray that they'll dig up enough evidence to clear me."

"I don't know why either of them would tell you anything."

"Don't you?" he said. "Well, when a guy gets a choice of having his head kicked in or of talking, you'd be surprised how chatty he can be. Especially after the first few licks. I know Cappy and Domenic. They're like a lot of other guys, awful tough until they're licked. If I had a gun I'd go after them now and take my chances, and you could scram in the car."

"You're thinking of some other girl," Holly said. "I'm the one who's staying with you, remember?"

He said irritably, "Wake up, Snow White. You're talking in your sleep."

"There's something wrong with that Snow White picture. I don't see any Prince Charming around. All I see is a man who thinks he's a lone wolf but acts like a stranded puppy."

"I can take care of myself."

"Maybe so. But I don't think you can take care of your two murdering friends."

"Your scheme involved watching for people following me, didn't it? Where were you when the gray sedan came into sight?"

"I was busy thinking up reasons why you need help. I can't do a million things at once. Bill, you *do* need help."

"Sorry. Your scheme is out."

"You're not going to get rid of me just by saying that."

"I'm going to do more than say it. I'm going to drive you to the hotel in Yosemite Valley and put you out of the car and leave. If I have to use force, okay."

"I dare you to try that! If you put me out of the car, or sneak away, I'm going to the police with the whole story."

He laughed. "That's a big bluff. First you want to help me and then you threaten to turn me in to the cops."

"It's not a bluff. And I wouldn't be doing it to get you in trouble. I'd be doing it to get you out of trouble. Cappy and Domenic are nice and handy so the police can grab them. We can prove they trailed us from Reno. We can prove they tried to kill us in an accident. With that much to go on, maybe the police can prove Cappy and Domenic were in Cheyenne and Salt Lake City and did the other murders."

"Are you serious? Why would the cops give up an airtight case against me just because we asked them please to pin it on two other guys?"

"You'd have a better chance if you were arrested than if you went after Cappy and Domenic alone. That would merely get you killed. So you'll be smart to take my first offer and let me help."

She had a soft rounded chin but right now it looked as if it could plow stumps from the ground. Apparently she meant all this. "Everybody has a natural urge for self-preservation," he said. "Let me appeal to yours. If I okayed your scheme, that alibi I worked out for you would be wrecked. The whole thing depends on you ditching me as soon as you can. If you went on with me, it would look as though you were helping me get away with murder."

"Let me appeal to *your* sense of self-preservation. Besides the help I can give you, I'm the only witness who can back up your story. If I used that alibi you invented, and if you were arrested, I'd be a witness against you."

"You couldn't clear me in a trial. A smart prosecutor would tear you to bits."

"Oh, I don't know," she said. "He couldn't make me admit anything but that you're stupid, pig-headed, stubborn, shortsighted and rude. As far as I know there are no laws against those things. Not that there shouldn't be."

Obviously he couldn't talk her out of this. But he couldn't let her go with him or call in the police. If she tagged along with him she'd be in constant danger. If she called in the cops, they'd accuse her of being an accessory after the fact of three murders. Either way she'd be in a bad jam. The idea was to fix things so she wouldn't be in a jam at all. He had to trick her into walking out on him and never wanting to see him again. He thought he saw how it could be done. His plan would take a while to work and it would make him look like a heel, but that didn't matter. He let out a carefully toned laugh, with just the right amount of amusement and admiration in it, and said, "You're quite a girl." He put an arm around her and pulled her close.

She held herself so rigidly that she felt about as cuddly as a sack of rocks. "What's all this for?" she asked.

"Why don't you relax? Hasn't a man ever put his arm around you before?"

"Certainly. Where do you think I was brought up, in a tomb?"

"That may be it. You act slightly dead."

"The only other time you ever grabbed me was this morning. You were trying to teach me a lesson."

"Maybe I learned one myself."

"Bill, it isn't safe to do any one-arm driving on this road."

"Glad you reminded me," he said, stopping the car.

She looked very startled. He grinned and began to kiss her. She didn't struggle or respond in any way. He opened one eye and peeked. Her eyes were only an inch away and they were wide open and looked enormous. This was working out very well; his plan would have fallen apart if she had liked this. He let his lips brush over her chin and down the line of her throat.

"Bill," she said, "there's a car coming."

He straightened, and she zipped to the far side of the seat like a released spring. He listened for the car, didn't hear anything. He said, "You needn't think I can't reach that far."

"A car *will* come," she protested. "Maybe the gray sedan. Please let's go."

He had made a good beginning. If he rushed things

she might get suspicious. He started the car and drove on again.

Holly said in an uncertain tone, "You haven't said anything more about my plan."

"I'm thinking about it," he said, flicking a glance at her. "From a new angle." She looked away, and he saw a large gulp go down her throat. If she was worried already, wait till he turned on the heat.

In another half-hour they reached the top of the pass and cruised by a snow field and coasted through the stone gateway to Yosemite National Park. He bought a ticket from the Ranger on duty and said he had no firearms. That gave him the idea of updating the plant inspection station trick.

"We passed a gray sedan on the way up here," he said. "Couple of guys in it were taking pot shots at gophers or something up in the rocks. I don't think that sort of stuff ought to be allowed."

"We don't allow it in the Park. Guns have to be sealed or broken down so they can't be used. These two men are headed this way?"

"Yes. Their car looks as if it had been in an accident."

The Ranger glanced at the left side of the convertible. "Didn't have any trouble with them, did you?"

He couldn't afford to get the Rangers in this. "No. No trouble."

"We'll make sure their guns are out of business," the man said.

Bill drove on. Sealing their guns wouldn't put Cappy and Domenic out of business, but at least it would delay them. On top of the delay caused by damage to their car, it ought to leave them far behind and give him plenty of time to work on Holly. He drove along a two-lane road for a few miles through mountain meadows and then plunged into forests where the road went native on him. Except for turnouts here and there it was only wide enough for one car, and it went squirming through the trees like an Indian trail. The Ranger had given him a map showing that this trail went on for about twenty miles. They were going to be the longest miles the girl beside him had ever traveled. He stretched out an arm and scooped her in.

She trembled and said, "Not on this road, Bill, please."

"I'm not going off the road at twenty an hour, which is all I can make here. No drops to worry about, either."

"I'm not quite used to you acting like this."

"You'll never get accustomed to it if I quit," he said cheerily. He stopped the car and kissed her again. This time she began struggling. He lifted his head and put a little thickness in his voice and said, "You don't think I can cruise around with a gorgeous kid like you and just think how swell you'd look across a checkerboard, do you?"

"I don't know," she gasped. "You ought to have

some control. It's not as if we were the least bit in love or anything."

"What's love got to do with it?"

"It makes things like this very different," she said, as if blurting out a memorized lesson. "When you're in love you want to do anything you can for the other person and…and making love is one of the ways, although of course it's for yourself too and—"

"You make it sound like medicine. Now look. I haven't decided about your plan yet. But if you're going to act like this, I'll tell you right now it won't work. You better loosen up a bit."

"I'll…try," she said weakly.

He kissed her a couple more times and got a very cold reaction; she squeezed her eyes shut and grimaced like a kid taking castor oil. As a mastermind who had planned it this way he liked that reaction. As a plain ordinary run-of-the-human-race man it annoyed hell out of him. He let her go finally and drove on, taking deep angry breaths.

She picked the wrong reason for his deep breathing, and said, "Do you often lose control like this?"

"Only," he snapped, "when I'm with a girl."

"Would it help get you back to normal if I told you about some of this wonderful country we're driving through? For instance—"

"No," he said, and reached for her.

She retreated to the farthest corner of the seat and

said rapidly, "I'm going to tell you anyway and I bet it will help. That was the eastern face of the Sierras we climbed on our way to Tioga Pass. The eastern face is much steeper than the western face. After the Sierras were formed, the eastern face faulted and a huge mass of land dropped straight down leaving the eastern face very sheer."

"That reminds me," he said. "You'd look nice in something sheer."

"No I wouldn't! I'm much too skinny. Besides we were talking about mountains. Most of the rock here is granite. It—"

"It reminds me of you," he said, gathering her in successfully this time.

She crouched inside the curve of his arm and talked rapidly. After a few miles she ran out of geology and looked around nervously for another subject. They were still winding down through the forest so that suggested botany. She reported that within Yosemite National Park were sixteen of the forty-three cone-bearing trees of California. Forty percent in this one little area, think of that! He thought of that and slowed for a second and kissed her and she went into high gear about ponderosa pines and incense cedars. If he had been making a serious pass at her he would have been ready to start a forest fire. She had a good defense with all that chatter. It was very difficult to get steamed up about a girl who tells you that the giant sequoia has fireproof bark which sometimes grows two feet thick, and wood containing a lot of tannin, all of which discourages insects and helps the sequoia live to a ripe old age.

When you listened to that for a while you began to reach a ripe old age too.

He kept making little mechanical passes at her, however. She was so upset that she didn't realize they were mechanical. They had quite a lively drive for the next hour. Then they left the virgin timber and hit a good two-lane road and made a long curve south and finally a tremendous view began opening up on the right. He drove into a parking area and looked out over Yosemite Valley. Old Mother Nature had really cut loose here. You could picture her bustling around like a woman rearranging a living room, draping a few thousand feet of waterfall here and pushing a mile-high cliff there and carpeting the place with a hundred-foot thickness of trees and then deciding maybe that mountain peak ought to be over in *that* corner and—

"It takes your breath away, doesn't it?" Holly said.

She would be sorry she reminded him of business. He glanced around, saw that no other cars were in sight. "You take my breath away," he said.

She saw the look in his eyes and began stammering that the big cliff on the left was El Capitan, seven thousand five hundred and sixty-four feet, and that the huge one in the distance was Half Dome, and then she ran out of words except for no and please don't and stop. He went right ahead giving her a pretty complete mauling. She had a lovely body and it was lucky she didn't like the pawing because with any encourage-ment he could have worked up a real interest in it. Even as it was, he had some trouble. One part of his mind coached him in a cool detached way while the other part acted like a cheering section.

He released her at last when she began to cry. She ought to have a clear idea, by now, of what she would have to take if she teamed up with him. And if that wasn't enough to send her bawling back to the first grade, here was something more.

"You know what?" he said. "I'm going to check out of this rat race."

She choked off a sob and said faintly, "What exactly do you mean?"

"I mean this business of playing hide-and-go-seek with cops, and trying to nail Cappy and Domenic before they nail me. What's the percentage in it?"

"I don't understand you, Bill. The percentage is that you have a chance to clear yourself."

"I can clear myself like a guy with a penknife can cut down all these trees. I've been kidding myself. This thing gets worse as I go on. I'm going to check out."

"But you can't!" she cried. "The police will be after you for murder. Those two men will keep on trying to kill you. So—"

"Let's be sensible. The only cop who knows the score is that cowboy of yours. He can't say too much because he'd look silly, admitting that I smacked him down and walked off the way I did. The cops in Reno may never connect me with the killing. That leaves Cappy and Domenic. If I quit giving them trouble, why should they spend their lives hunting me?"

"Bill, you'd never have an easy moment! You'd never know when something might go wrong. You couldn't get a job and settle down."

"Who wants to settle down in some dull job?"

"How are you going to live?"

"To start with," he said, "there's this car and about five thousand bucks."

"It wouldn't last forever."

This was the place for the payoff line. "On top of that, I have a one-third interest in a jackpot of five hundred thousand bucks."

"But that's the money in the plane that crashed! How could you get it away from those two men? How—" She stopped, looked at him in horror. "You don't mean you'd make a deal with them?"

"Why should they get it all? I have as much right to it as they have."

"Nobody has a right to it. That's stolen money. It—"

"Don't go legal on me. If it's a choice between taking stolen money or taking a murder rap, I don't have to say eenie-meenie-miney-mo to pick which."

"They'd kill you if you tried to make a deal!"

"Oh, I don't know. I ease up to them and say, look, fellows, let's call off the war. If anything happens to me, a friend of mine is going to mail a sealed envelope to the cops, and they'll have the whole story. It may not pin the murders on you guys but it sure will wash out your chance of getting the gold out of the plane. So let's make a deal. See, Holly? It works out nicely."

She swallowed a few times, looking as if she were gulping down broken glass. "I don't understand how it works out for me."

"It works out swell. The two of us team up. You ditch this tour and we play it together. We take our share of the gold and head for South America. How's it sound?"

Of course he knew exactly how it sounded. It sounded like a guy having a nightmare and offering to let her in on it. It sounded like a rat saying: let's set up housekeeping in the sewer, honey. Judging by the look on her face it made her pretty sick.

"Bill," she said in a choked voice, "I can't answer that right away. Could we drive to the hotel and let me think about it as we go?"

"Think about it?" he said, putting a lot of surprise in his voice. "I don't know what there is to think about. But just as you say."

They drove silently down into the valley and through cathedral columns of trees toward The Ahwahnee, where the Treasure Trip party would be staying. At any other time the soaring cliffs and trees and waterfalls would have impressed him, but right now they just seemed like a lot of rock and wood and water that had got out of hand and run wild. For all he cared they could shove a few mountains into the place and bulldoze everything flat and make something useful out of it, like a parking lot.

The Ahwahnee was a huge rambling hotel, huddled under cliffs that made it look like a matchbox. He drove to the entrance and stopped the car and waited to see how many words Holly would use in calling him a heel. She got out of the car and asked him to wait while she checked at the reception desk to make sure the Treasure Trip bus hadn't arrived yet. He shrugged. Maybe she wasn't going to use any words. Maybe she was going to send out a bellboy with word that she didn't want to see him any more.

In about ten minutes, however, she came out. Her face looked like a load of damp wash. "I want to make sure of one thing," she said. "Are you really serious about this?"

He let out a flat laugh. "I don't know anything more serious than wanting to stay alive and to get a cut of half a million in gold. What do you think?"

"I wish I could think that you're just tired and discouraged. There have been times before this when you wanted to quit, you know."

"Who's quitting? I've just started to play this right, that's all. What's wrong with you? Are you stalling?"

"I can't go with you, Bill."

"You were all set to run off with me before I saw the right way out of this mess. I don't get it."

"I thought you needed my help. But this way you don't."

He took her hand. It felt as if she had been storing it in one of the local glaciers. "I don't need your help," he said huskily. "What I need is you, baby. We could have ourselves a time."

Her hand trembled and she pulled it away. "I don't see it like that," she said. She gave him a fat white envelope, and added, "I wrote out a bill of sale for the car and had it notarized in the hotel. It's in here. Your money is in here too. Goodbye, Bill."

"I'll never understand it," he said. "I can't see what you've got to lose."

"Whatever it is," she said, "I think I've already lost it." She turned and hurried back into the hotel.

Well, that was that. Things had worked out exactly as he had planned. That was good. That was fine. He didn't know why he should feel so rotten about it.

Fifteen

He sat outside his redwood cabin on the grounds of The Ahwahnee and thought how it would startle Holly if she found out he was a neighbor of hers. But she wasn't going to find out, if he could help it. She was a smart kid and might ask why he couldn't tear himself away. She might even figure out the right answer, and realize that he had tricked her into walking out on him. Then she might want to play tag with murder again.

She was close enough to murder as things were. Cappy and Domenic knew she had been helping him. They probably felt she knew too much about them and the killings and the sunken gold. If he managed to slip away from them, they might decide to get rid of Holly before taking up the chase again. So he was sticking around for a while. The convertible was hidden in a far corner of one of the hotel's parking lots. That is, it was hidden from Holly, who had no special·reason to look for it, but it was where Cappy and Domenic ought to spot it easily. It was bait set out to show he was at the hotel, and to coax Cappy and Domenic to wait patiently.

He was planning a disappointment for them. A day

had already passed safely since Holly and he arrived in Yosemite Valley. After tonight and tomorrow and the next night, Holly would be leaving with the Treasure Trip tour. If the boys saw her leaving they might be upset, but they wouldn't chase her. They would hang around waiting for him. He planned to give Holly a day's start and then make a break for it in the convertible. If he got out of the Park in one piece he would buy a gun. For a change he was going to use it, too. He had given up those big ideas about making them talk and trying to clear himself. It was too risky. He was likely to make a mistake and let them knock him off. That wouldn't be much of a loss but it would put Holly back in the middle again.

Getting in The Ahwahnee without Holly knowing had been easy. After she left him late yesterday afternoon he had driven the car to the parking lot and sat in it until he saw the Treasure Trip bus arrive. He waited until he was sure all of them had checked in and gone to their rooms, then went to the hotel desk and asked for a room. He explained that he didn't have a reservation but hoped someone with a reservation hadn't shown up. The clerk checked his list and found that a man named William Wayne had not arrived with the Treasure Trip party to take the room reserved for him. Yes, the clerk said, that could take care of him. Bill thanked him and signed the register carefully: George H. Lawrence, of Santa Barbara, California.

He had figured on staying in his room nearly all the

time, to avoid being spotted by Holly or members of her party. But by luck he had managed to get one of the cabins in a grove of big trees near the hotel. That gave him a chance to move around as much as necessary. He had told one of the bellboys that he had quarreled with the girl in charge of the Treasure Trip party and wanted to hang around, without letting her know, until it looked like a good time to make up with her. In order to pick the right time, of course, he needed to know what she was doing and who she was running around with. A story like that required a certain amount of proof to convince a bellboy, and he had handed over twenty bucks worth of it. The bellboy kept him well informed. Last night, for example, Bill had been able to trail Holly when she went for a walk with a few other members of the party, and make sure nothing happened to her.

There was only one flaw in his plan. If any cops came around looking for him, they wouldn't have much trouble. But that was a minor point. If they trailed him to Yosemite it wouldn't matter where he hid in the Park. There were only four routes out and there was a Ranger station at each gateway. He could never get by if they were watching for him.

He saw somebody coming down the winding path to the cabin colony. He kept close track of visitors, and watched carefully until he identified his bellboy.

The kid came up and said, "Evening, Mr. Lawrence. Did they bring you a good dinner?"

"Yes, it was fine. The tray's in the cabin any time a waiter wants to pick it up. Is Miss Clark through dinner in the dining room?"

"She won't be back for dinner."

"How come?"

"Well, you know she went sight-seeing with some of her party today. She and five others are staying up at Glacier Point Hotel for dinner and to watch the firefall, and they'll drive back afterward."

He could see Glacier Point from where he was sitting. It was across the Valley, a huge wedge of granite rearing up more than three thousand feet. Glacier Point Hotel was up there. If you had wings it was only a couple miles away. If you had wheels it was thirty miles by a winding mountain road.

He said nervously, "Isn't that a tough drive to make in the dark?"

"They have one of the hotel's cars and a chauffeur. To a guy who knows the road and takes it easy, that drive isn't bad at night. You don't have to worry, Mr. Lawrence."

"Okay," he muttered. He took out five dollars and gave it to the kid. "Let me know when she gets back."

He watched the bellboy vanish down the path to the hotel, and tried to read a couple of pamphlets on cone-bearing trees of the Park and on the Yosemite Indians. They didn't hold his interest. His glance kept wandering to the jutting mass of Glacier Point. Last night he had stood among the trees keeping an eye on

Holly, who was watching the firefall. High up on Glacier Point the Rangers built a fire and slowly pushed the embers over the cliff. The glowing torrent fell almost a thousand feet. That was a long drop.

The phone rang in his cabin. It threw his nerves into a short circut until he remembered that it might be somebody on the hotel staff calling on quite innocent business. He went in and picked it up.

"This is room service," a high-pitched voice said. "In regard to your order we—"

"My order came all right, thanks."

"Was everything satisfactory?"

"Yeah. Sure. Fine. You can pick the tray up any time."

The voice slid down a couple of notches. "Isn't that sweet? How about picking you up sometime, Bill?"

His hand locked around the phone until the knuckles creaked. "This is George H. Lawrence," he said hoarsely. "You have the wrong party."

The man snickered. "Don't give me that stuff, Bill. I ought to know your voice. I used to hear it enough over an intercom."

It was Domenic. The guy would love something like this. You could picture him cuddling up to the phone, eyelids drooping over hot black eyes, a smirk lifting the corner of his mouth. Domenic had been a good crew chief except he always wanted to make a big production out of whatever he did. This would be a wonderful chance for him.

"Hello, Domenic," he said. "I'd ask what's on your mind but I'm not sure you've got one."

"Don't be like that. After all the trouble I had locating you. Would your lousy hotel give out any information? No. So what do I do? I call up and say as I was driving out of the parking lot I happened to nick the fender of a convertible. I don't know whose it is but here's the license number and I'll be glad to send the owner a check for the damage. So they finally say they'll connect me with a guy named Lawrence and I pull that room service gag to make sure it's you. Cute, huh?"

"Yeah. Swell. Hang on a moment, Domenic." He put down the phone and took a quick look outside the cabin. Nobody was in sight. No figure was slipping toward him through the trees. He went back into the cabin. "Okay," he said. "Go on telling me how smart you are."

"Little nervous, huh, Bill? Making sure Cappy wasn't peeking over your shoulder? Relax. We have no idea what room you're in."

"I wouldn't advise you to come sneaking around anyway."

"What would we sneak for, Bill? We got nothing to hide. Besides, all we want is a little talk with you. Maybe we can iron things out."

"Go ahead and talk. I'm listening."

"We can't settle this over a phone. How about sitting down with Cappy and me?"

"I'll think it over."

"How about tonight, Bill?"

"I won't have my thinking done that fast."

"Don't play so hard to get," Domenic said softly. "Let's make it tonight. Up at Glacier Point."

The telephone began to get slippery with sweat from his hand. "That's a long way off."

"It's not so far…straight down."

He gripped the telephone as if he had Domenic's throat. "What are you trying to say? If you have some idea that—"

"Wait a minute, w-a-i-t a minute, Bill. We just think you ought to get up to see Glacier Point. They build a fire for the firefall right out close to the edge. They have iron railings around the edge but if a person ever slipped he could go right under the bottom rail. There's always a little crowd up there watching the firefall and of course there are no lights except the fire and flashlights and it's a wonder nobody ever falls. You know how careless people can get, running around not looking where they're going. Do you know any careless people, Bill?"

It could be a coincidence that Holly was up there too. It was possible that Domenic and Cappy didn't know she was there. But the mocking note in Domenic's voice said it was no coincidence and that they knew all about the girl. "No," he said trying for that million-to-one shot, "I don't know any careless people. Do you?"

Domenic murmured, "She's right out there now leaning over the edge."

His stomach felt as if it were falling through space. "All right," he said thickly. "I'll come up."

"It's just about eight, Bill. It's a thirty-mile drive. The firefall is at nine. Maybe around nine-thirty there might be another fall, if you're not here."

"Where will I meet you?"

"You can park near Glacier Point Hotel. That's close to the firefall. It'll be dark by then. Sit in your car and blink your lights on and off three times. Repeat it every minute or so until we show up."

"All right. I'll see you."

"Just one thing more," Domenic said. "There's only one telephone line coming up here. Cappy's gonna take it out as soon as I hang up. So don't bother calling."

The phone clicked in his ear. He signaled for the operator, got her, asked for Glacier Point Hotel. There was a long wait filled with static from the phone and the waterfall roar of blood in his head. The operator came back finally and said, "There must be some trouble on the line. Will you try a little later?"

He said no thanks and dropped the phone and ran out of the cabin. He couldn't help looking off and up to his left. Glacier Point leaned over the valley as if ready to topple into it: billions of tons of sheer granite with long gray scars where embers had burned away the darker lichens. It would be a nice safe job. You

would walk up behind a girl in the dark, after the firefall was over, and slug her in the head with a rock and
roll her over the edge. Afterward nobody could prove
which rock hit her first.

Of course this was an obvious trap. Cappy and
Domenic had fixed up one of those deals where one
party to a dispute goes away satisfied and the other
goes away dead. Maybe they had set a trap along the
winding mountain road to Glacier Point. Or maybe
they would let him have it when he reached the place.
He had made a mistake thinking they would sit back
waiting for him to make the first move. They had
worked out a very nice double-or-nothing offer: see if
you can win your girl back without both of you getting
killed.

He ran down the path to the hotel and into the
lobby, looking for his bellboy. He spotted him at the
entrance, ran up to him and said, "You got a car?
Here?"

"Yeah, sure, Mr. Lawrence. Something wrong with
yours?"

"I want to rent yours for tonight. Hundred bucks.
Okay?"

"Yes, sir! I'll bring it right around."

"Swell. Make it fast."

He stood at the entrance, sweating, until the
bellboy drove up in a battered coupe. He handed the
kid his money, jumped in.

For the first fifteen minutes he had to drive at a

maddeningly slow rate through the traffic of the valley. Then he reached the Wawona Road slicing up the south wall of the valley and began driving fast. The car was much lighter than the big convertible and on some of the turns it wanted to take off like a kite. He roared through the long Wawona Tunnel and reached the turn-off to Glacier Point and skidded into it. It was twenty to nine.

The road burrowed through trees where night came early. He had fifteen miles to go. That wouldn't have been much on the flat but the only flatness up here was straight up and down. Driving fast on this road was like wrestling with a judo expert. Sometimes the road twisted and wrenched at the car. Sometimes it flopped limply in front of him to coax him to relax and then tried a bone-breaking series of tricks. Every now and then he almost lost the road and saw his headlights fan over green blankness and by instinct twitched the wheel the right way and got back on the beam. The best thing was that Cappy and Domenic weren't watching for a battered coupe. The worst thing was that he wasn't averaging thirty miles an hour. He broke out of the trees finally and into a bare dark world. Up ahead lights pricked holes in the blackness. The road swung toward them and threw one last skidding curve at him and then tied itself into a meek loop in front of the hotel. He jammed on brakes, jumped out, ran up a path toward the top of Glacier Point. The firefall was over and people with flashlights were straggling back to the hotel. He reached the summit, looked for Holly. The flashlights had fogged his eyes and it was hard to see. Here and there people moved and talked—a dozen of them, maybe—and any one of them could be Holly. Any of them could be Cappy or Domenic. He didn't have time to waste.

"Holly!" he called sharply. "Holly!"

Way off an echo bounced back at him. That was all. His tongue felt like an old hunk of cloth gagging his mouth. This couldn't be it. An echo couldn't be all that was left of a bright-haired girl who skipped through life as happily as a kid at recess. He took a deep breath to yell again.

A hand came out of the darkness. A soft warm hand that pressed against his mouth and stopped the yell. A girl whispered, "Bill! Be quiet!"

He grabbed her arms, stared down into the pale oval of her face. "Holly?" he said. "It's you?"

"Of course it's me! You're crazy, coming here screaming my name. I thought you were somewhere safe by now. Don't you—"

He shook her a little. "Shut up," he said. "They laid a trap for you. Cappy and Domenic. You were going over the edge in a few minutes. We've got to get out of here."

"And…you came back for me?"

"I didn't go away. I've been at the hotel all along, trying to keep an eye on you. I was afraid they'd try something. Come on!"

She gasped, "You've got to listen to me first. Carson Smith is up here. And that sheriff of his from Cheyenne. They've been spying on me. They must be waiting for you to show up. And Bill, they must have heard you call my name."

"Where are they right now?"

"They were here a little while ago. It's hard to tell now in the dark. I can't see anything. Can you?"

He took a careful look around Glacier Point. Nobody was within a hundred feet of them at the moment. That is, nobody he could see. But the place was studded with black lumps that could be rocks or crouching men. Maybe they could make a dash back to the car, maybe they couldn't. He made a sudden decision and picked the girl up in his arms.

"Bill," she whispered, "What are you doing? What—"

"We're going to find the sheriff."

Her body tensed in his arms. "You can't. He'll arrest you."

"Don't give me an argument. I should have done this a couple days ago. This is no game for you to be playing. Remember to tell the cops that story I worked out for you and you'll be in the clear."

"Put me down! I won't have you doing this. I—"

She struggled a little. He tightened his grip and let her squirm. After a few moments she began crying, went limp. He started walking toward the nearest people. Cappy and Domenic might be up here but they would never suspect a man carrying a girl in his arms; they would be looking for two people running. The first people he approached turned out to be strangers. He headed toward another couple and then, quite a way beyond, saw a couple of shadowy figures wearing broad-brimmed hats. They were leaning against the railing that fenced off the big drop. He stumbled toward them and when he came close saw a glint of starlight on badges and holstered guns. Good. It was a relief to get this over.

"Hello, sheriff," he said. "This is Wayne. Looking for me?"

The shadows jerked as if he had stabbed them.

Carson Smith said, "Well, can yuh tie that!"

"What did I tell you, Carse?" the sheriff said. "I told you if we watched this girl we'd get Wayne. But I shore didn't think it'd be like this. Tired of hiding, Wayne?"

"I'm tired of getting this girl in a jam. She's on the level, see? She was trying to help me and didn't know the score. Right now a couple of guys are gunning for me and I don't want her to catch any bullets by mistake. This is the only way to make sure she doesn't."

"Well, now," the sheriff said, "that's mighty noble of you, Wayne. Just stand there quiet while we see are you heeled."

"Yep," Carson Smith said. "Mighty noble."

There was something queer about the way Smith said that. Bill peered at him. He saw the guy reach lazily for his gun and lift it and bring the barrel down in a glittering arc across the back of the sheriff's neck. The sheriff dropped without a sound.

"Mighty noble," Smith said, crouching. "Now let's see what it will get you."

Sixteen

This ought to be a bad dream. It was only in bad dreams that you did the right and logical thing and found it was horribly wrong and stupid. Maybe in a moment somebody would wake him and tell him to stop screaming. You didn't remember bad dreams very long. A few hours after awaking there wouldn't be much left except a vague memory of a haunted top-of-the-world landscape where one had almost been caught by faceless things.

Nobody was going to wake him this time, though. He had to yank himself back to reality. He started slowly, pinning his attention on small understandable things: the way starlight smeared on the barrel of Carson Smith's revolver, the thin stripes of the railing against black space, the glint of a ring on the sheriff's limp right hand.

He heard Holly say to the man in front of them, "You must be mad!"

"Yeah?" Smith said softly.

"You can't hate Bill this much," she said.

"No?"

He was awake again. This was real and made sense. Answers were clicking into place in his mind like the wheels of a slot machine. Click: the first wheel stopped on China. Click: the second wheel stopped on Philadelphia. Click: Glacier Point. He could have hit this jackpot long ago if he had done some hard thinking. But there had been a sign in his head announcing: Quiet, please. Brain at rest. Holly had given him the answer long ago but he hadn't paid any attention. There *had* been a sixth guy in the crooked deal that started back in China. It was Carson Smith.

"You can't get away with it," he said huskily. "A dozen people are in earshot. A couple must be Rangers. Pull that trigger and you invite them over."

"You're wanted for murder," Smith said. "There's a warrant out for you. Jump me and I got a right to shoot."

Holly gasped, "How can he jump you? He—"

"Shut up," Bill said. "You don't get the idea. Look, Smith, it'll be messy. You can explain a bullet in me. But you'll have trouble explaining one in her."

"Will I?"

"I'm going to put her down," Bill said. "I don't have a gun. I'm not going to make any sudden moves. Don't you make any either. Now listen, Holly. Move slow and easy. Don't make a sound unless he jumps us. But if he does, scream and run."

"Watch it, Wayne," Smith said, his voice starting to rise. "Watch it."

Brother, he was watching it. This was like teasing a rattler. They had only one thing in their favor: Smith didn't want noise. Bill tensed to catch the first flicker of action from the crouching man. He bent his knees slowly and let his arms down until Holly's feet touched rock and the weight eased off his arms. She straightened carefully and stood up and he put an arm in front of her body and moved her a slow step to one side. He wasn't quite sure how he had managed to get away with it. A couple of times Smith had teetered right on the edge of leaping. But something had held him back. Something—

Bill said, "We're moving straight ahead to the railing. Jump us and you'll get screams."

"Stay right there," Smith snapped. "I'll plug you."

Bill took a deep breath and tried to let it out in slow calm words. "You won't plug us," he said. "What have you got to lose by waiting? This place is getting more deserted every minute. All we want to do is take four steps to the railing and turn around and talk. So you don't want to shoot. Come on, Holly. Very slowly. One step. That's right. As long as we don't yell you're okay, Smith. We aren't going to yell if we don't have to. Now a second step. Easy now. A third. In fifteen minutes there won't be anybody around to bother you, Smith. So take it easy. Now the fourth step. There. Now we keep watching Smith and turn with our backs to the railing. That's it." He let the last bit of breath hiss from aching lungs. Sweat stung his skin. He hadn't thought they would make it.

"Got away with it, didn't you?" Smith said.

"Yeah. Thanks. I don't like people sneaking up behind me. You want to call Cappy and Domenic now?"

Beside him Holly started to tremble. "Oh no," she whispered.

"Wise guy," Smith said, spitting out the words. He raised his voice slightly. "Come on, you dopes."

Two shadows stirred in the rocks twenty feet away, edged forward.

Bill called softly. "Don't rush us. We aren't going over this railing without a lot of noise."

"I think I've gone crazy," Holly said in a choked voice. "Those two men and Carson and...and what does it all mean?"

"It's kind of complicated," Bill said. "Hello, Cappy. Hello, Domenic. Stop there or I'll yell."

The two shadows paused, five feet away.

"What a mess," Smith said furiously. "You let Wayne slip right by you in the parking lot. You take hours sneaking up behind him."

"He came in another car," Domenic said. "How could we know?"

Cappy said, "How could we sneak up on him when you couldn't make him stay put?"

Smith growled, "What do I do, shoot him and bring a crowd, or jump him and get yells that bring a crowd?"

"Jeez," Domenic said. "How far can a guy parlay a couple yells?"

Yeah. Bill thought, how far? You could parlay them

for a few minutes, that was all. And by then maybe the few people left on the crest of Glacier Point would have wandered back to the hotel and the yells wouldn't buy any attention. Still and all, who wanted to throw away the last ten or fifteen minutes of life? Something might happen. An earthquake might jolt Smith and Domenic and Cappy over the cliff. They might get religion. He might point his finger at them and say bang and will them dead. Anyway the important thing was to talk. Talk fast. Talk them off balance.

"What have you got to lose?" he said. "We can't run. We know that the second we yell for help, you let us have it. Don't sneak in on me, Cappy!"

Cappy pulled back his foot. "You don't bluff me," he muttered.

"One of you do some thinking, will you?" Smith said angrily.

"I'm doing some," Domenic said. "My thinking says take it easy. I see you cooled off the sheriff."

"Got any objections?" Smith asked.

"Yeah," Domenic said. "This starts to get too whole-sale for me. First it's just Bill we're after. Then his dame. Now the sheriff."

"I had to do it," Smith said. "The minute Wayne spills his story, our lake deal gets wrecked. I told you this afternoon you had to get Wayne before the sheriff caught him."

"Aah, you shouldn't have let the sheriff get wind of it at all," Domenic growled.

"Let him?" Smith said. "There wasn't any letting about it. The sheriff dug around all by himself and found Russ did know Ken and Frankie. That showed him I was riding a hot trail. I'd phoned him from Reno I was coming here so he knew where to find me. I couldn't stall him off. I had to tell him I was after Wayne."

Holly said faintly, "I'm not just imagining all this? Carson has been working with them all along?"

"Sure," Bill said. "He's the mystery man you tried to sell me and I wouldn't buy it. He was the sixth man in the gang. The organizer. The guy who made all the decisions. The guy I didn't know about. His dumb cowboy act was a fake. He sounds a lot smarter now, doesn't he?"

He stopped. Somewhere in the distance a voice called, "Hol-lee. Hol-lee."

"That's one of our party," Holly gasped. "They're ready to go back. They—"

"Hold it," Bill said, gripping her arm. She was working up to hysterics. She wanted to scream. But she wouldn't get out half a scream right now. "Call back to them nice and easy," he said. "Tell them you'll be along in five minutes."

Not many girls could have done it. She took a deep shuddering breath and called, "I'll be there in five minutes."

The distant voice called, "We'll be at the car." Echoes trundled the sound back and forth and let it fade away.

The sense of being in a dream was creeping over him again. That wouldn't do. He fixed his attention on the small understandable things once more: the way starlight smeared on the barrel of Carson Smith's revolver, the way the railing cut into his back, the glint of the ring on the sheriff's limp right hand. They helped bring him back to reality. They...wait a minute. What glint of what ring? He peered at the sheriff's body. There was no glint. Of course he had moved since he first noticed the ring catching starlight so probably he was in the wrong spot to see the reflection. He ought to be able to see the limp hand, though. It couldn't have—

The shakes hit him. He leaned back hard against the railing so his legs wouldn't fold. Nice work, Wayne. You play a cool game when there isn't a chance of winning and you come unstitched at the seams now. The sheriff's hand wasn't lying limply on the rock any more. It was back in the shadow of his body. It was inching toward his holster. Get in there and pitch, Wayne.

"Maybe we can make a deal," he said huskily. "What's the sense of a lot of killing?"

Domenic spat. "Look who's talking," he said. "Killer Wayne himself. The guy who's been going around knocking off my pals."

"The funny thing is," Bill said carefully, "you got the wrong guy. Am I gonna make you sore if I talk a little, Smith?"

"I wouldn't know," Smith said. He backed away a few steps.

"It shouldn't make you sore that I finally figured out what a smart guy you are," Bill said. "You were in China, weren't you? And you were in Nanking when the Nationalists started pulling out. At a guess, you'd been working with that Chinese black market guy who was in our plane that day. Anyway you knew the guy had a lot of gold in those medical supply boxes, and you sold my bunch the idea of grabbing it. When I threw a wrench in the works, you threw a slug into me. Right?"

Cappy said, "It took you a long time to catch on."

"I admit it. But nobody ever tipped me off that Smith had been in China."

Holly said weakly, "I could have told you that. But I never realized it meant anything. That first afternoon I met Carson, we happened to get talking about chop suey and he said he didn't think it was a real Chinese dish because he had never been able to get it over there. I forgot all about it until now. I'm sorry."

"That's all right," Bill said. "You couldn't know. Did you ever sweat about that little mistake, Smith?"

"I don't do much sweating," Smith said.

"Not even when you shot at me in Philadelphia and merely nicked my side?"

Domenic said, "What's this about a shooting in Philly?"

"You have a lot to learn," Bill said. "Russ got a newspaper clipping about me being alive and back home, and probably showed it to Smith. So Smith came to Philadelphia to get me. But he missed. Then he did some good detective work and found I was heading west on a tour through Cheyenne and Salt Lake City and Reno and Frisco and L.A. So he went back to Cheyenne to wait for me."

"Look, Carse," Domenic said. "Is that on the level?"

Smith had backed off about ten feet now. He crouched, balancing carefully. "What difference does it make?"

Bill glanced at the sheriff. He couldn't see the hand at all now. The sheriff's body had changed position slightly. Things were going to crack open fast. He hoped the sheriff had the word. "The difference," he said, "is Smith saw what a swell chance that was to get rid of five guys named Russ and Ken and Frankie and Cappy and Domenic. He thought I'd do the job for him and take the rap. But I didn't do the job and so he stepped in. That left me still taking the rap."

Cappy said harshly, "You better tell this guy off, Carse."

"He's waiting for me to finish telling you how smart he's been," Bill said. He gripped the girl's arm, got ready to spin her out of the way. "He phoned you guys from Salt Lake City or maybe Winnemucca, told you I'd killed Russ and Ken and was heading for Frankie in Reno. I'm guessing this but I'll bet it's close to what happened. He said meet him in Reno to knock me off. But what he was going to do was knock me off and then shoot you two. How close am I, Smith?"

Smith said softly, "You're close to a drop of three thousand feet."

"Answer him, will you?" Cappy said. "I don't like the sound of that. I—"

"How do you like the sound of this?" Smith said.

Flame split the night. Short ugly squirts of flame jabbing at Cappy and Domenic. Bill spun the girl around and off to the side and turned to lunge at Smith. It wasn't going to work. Cappy and Domenic were down in a heap and Smith was waiting for him. Waiting in a crouch, grinning, taking a second to enjoy this. Flame gushed again. Not from where he expected. Not from the gun in Smith's right hand. It came from the sheriff. And all of a sudden there wasn't a gun in Smith's right hand and the guy's arm flopped limp and he let out a sound you couldn't hear in the tumbling echoes and leaped forward.

Bill threw a right. It splashed on the guy's face, rocked him. He chopped quick hooks and battered the guy backward. Smith slammed him against the railing with a wild left swing and then came charging in fast. Bill ducked, jerked aside. The big lunging body crashed into the railing and went toppling over it. A scream rushed away into blackness. It went away fast. It ended far away in just a few seconds, but for quite a while you could hear one mountain peak whispering to another about it.

He wanted to lean over the railing and look down into that soft black comfortable space but a girl and a tired old guy wearing a badge hauled him back.

Seventeen

He drove slowly back down the twisting road from Glacier Point. For the last five miles he had been telling himself not to be a fool but he didn't seem to have an attentive audience. He had just managed to get rid of one load of trouble and now he seemed to want to go shopping for more. This time it wasn't killer trouble. It was girl trouble. He had suddenly realized that he didn't want Holly Clark to go skipping out of his life.

If he had been smart he could have seen this thing sneaking up on him all during the past week. Of course it was against his principles to be smart. Instead of making a careful play for the girl he had been scrapping with her. The two of them had been getting along like a dull razor meeting a tough beard. This was going to be the kind of romance that would need a referee more than a minister.

He glanced at Holly, sitting over at the far side of the front seat. Most people looked older when they were tired but Holly looked younger. Right now, she looked as if her parents ought to tuck her in bed with her favorite doll. He ought to say something to cheer her up.

"Tired?" he asked.

She nodded.

He was really at his best tonight. He wanted to cheer up a girl who had just seen three men killed and who had almost been killed too and so he asked if she was tired. He said, "You've had a tough time." That was good, too.

Holly said, "Do you suppose we'll have to stay around long for the inquest or whatever they have?"

"It shouldn't take very long. They have a U.S. Commissioner here who can handle it. And the sheriff makes a good witness to what happened."

"Bill, it was wonderful the way you figured everything out."

"Wonderful? I was stupid not to figure things out sooner, especially with you telling me to look for a sixth man. Smith was always hanging around, keeping an eye on me to make sure nothing went wrong. That should have made me start thinking. I should have got suspicious over the little tricks he kept pulling to make me sweat. He got a kick out of it. That's the mark of a real killer."

"Why didn't you give up the whole thing in Salt Lake City, when you realized that somebody was using you as his license for murder?"

"I've forgotten. That seems years ago. Maybe I just figured I could outsmart the guy."

"Did it have anything to do with a girl named Holly Clark? Who had managed to get herself all tangled up in the case? And who might get in trouble if you didn't stay around?"

He wished he could say yes. It would be a nice cheap way of playing hero and making a little time with her. But to be honest, he didn't know. His ideas about the girl had been very confused back in Salt Lake City. "It's hard to remember," he muttered. "Probably I was only thinking about myself."

"Oh, naturally. And of course you were only thinking about yourself when you tricked me into walking out on you, yesterday afternoon. And when you hung around the hotel keeping an eye on me. And when you came roaring up to Glacier Point tonight to stop them from throwing me over the edge."

"Well, I—"

"It was very nice of you and now we're all even and you don't owe me a thing," she said rapidly.

She talked too fast for him. About the time he was ready to say hello she had reached goodbye. This was going to be a very difficult project. "When we get through with the inquest," he said, "I'd like to—"

"I know. You'll be off to dive for that gold."

"Please let me finish my sentences."

"Yes, of course, Bill. But that's what you will do, isn't it?"

"After this story gets printed and they locate that lake, anybody visiting the place will have to bring along his own water if he wants room to swim. The hell with it. I couldn't get there first and it isn't mine anyway. Besides, I have a job lined up with an airline and I'd like to get started on it."

"Oh. Then what were you going to say?"

The car rolled into the long Wawona Tunnel just then, and the noise of tires and engine built up to a loud steady throb. He didn't think he would start making his pitch yet. There were a lot of echoes in the tunnel and when she said no he didn't want to keep hearing it for the next half-mile. He reached the end of the tunnel and drove into the parking space just beyond. Spread out before them was Yosemite Valley with its cliffs rearing up like surf. A last-quarter moon was lifting over the Sierras and plating the valley with black and silver.

He had prepared quite a speech but he forgot it and said angrily, "The way you've been acting since that hassle up on Glacier Point, you might think I was the one planning to push you over."

"That's interesting. How should I have acted?"

He had started off wrong and he might as well stumble ahead. "According to the books," he growled, "you should have flung yourself into my arms or something."

She laughed: a tiny waterfall of sound. "I can just see little Holly flinging herself at Bill Wayne and Mr. Wayne dodging cleverly and little Holly going out over the valley in a swan dive."

He said in a burst of irritation, "I don't get it. I didn't have the slightest trouble making passes at you, when I was doing it to make you walk out on me. But now I don't know how to go about it. This time I don't want you to walk out, see?"

"Oh dear. Do I have to start bobbing and weaving again? Should I tell you that Half Dome is eight thousand eight hundred and fifty-two feet high and—"

"What a life this is going to be," he muttered. "Every time I have a romantic thought, she'll read me a back issue of the National Geographic."

"Bill, are you trying to say what I think you're trying to say?"

"You've been tagging around after me for years. Now I want to start tagging around after you."

She stared at him for a moment and then said quickly, "I think you have the wrong idea about me. I am *not* helplessly in love with you. I told you once that you were just a challenge to me, like a jigsaw puzzle that's hard to work but that you can't leave alone. I told you when I finished it I'd want to kick the thing into a million pieces."

"Go ahead and kick. I don't break up easily."

"Bill, be sensible. You've been out of the country for years. I'm the first American girl you've spent any time with, so naturally you're sort of attracted. On top of that you feel I helped you and you're grateful. That's all very nice but it doesn't add up to love."

"Your reasoning is brilliant. Only trouble is, it's wrong."

"See how we argue all the time? That's no basis for marriage."

"You're so right. But we can solve that easily. You can stop arguing."

She patted his cheek and said, "Be a good boy and go back to Philadelphia and take that airline job. Get that gorgeous car repaired and polished, and go around visiting your friends and looking lonely and you'll be startled at what will happen. Girls will pop up from nowhere. Take your time and pick out the nicest one and marry her. What do you think of that program?"

"It's too sensible for me."

"Well, I'm sorry," she said. "Excuse me from having a grateful man around. When the gratitude wore off it would be awful."

"I am not one bit grateful," he snapped. "From the time you were a kid I've resented the way you tagged along. I resented the help you've been giving me. It's beyond me how I end up thinking you're wonderful. Go on. Play hard to get. I've just had a lot of practice chasing people."

"Of all the boastful statements! If you make as many mistakes chasing me as you did chasing Carson Smith, you won't get far. And don't forget, this time I won't be helping you."

"I won't make as many mistakes," he said grimly. "This time I know who I'm chasing."

He slid an arm around her and began pulling her close. She put up a struggle. Not as much as he would have expected, though. He grinned. It was quite possible that, if he started making too many mistakes, she would give him a little help this time too.